Something Just Ain't Right

SOMETHING JUST AIN'T RIGHT

First edition. February 7, 2021.

ISBN: 979-8223666318

Written by Sheena Binkley.

Table of Contents

Acknowledgements

Thank you God for gracing me with this amazing talent. You have brought me through so much and has guided me each and every day. Thank you, not just for this journey, but for everything You have done for me.

To my hubby, Ethan Faulkner: Thank you for being the person that you are. Even though my numerous rants, you have supported me and for that's something I truly cherish. Love you, babe!

To my family and friends: Thank you for your continuous support, even when I talk about my characters as if they are real people (sorry, but I love my characters!) You all are truly wonderful!

Laurencia Smith: Thank you for your advice and suggestions. Even through my indie days you was the first person I would ask advice about on various stories. I hope I'm able to do the same for you as you prepare for your first book as you have done for me. ☺

Shawnda Hamilton: Thank you everything you do. You have helped put my name out there. You have been extremely helpful and for that, I truly thank you.

To the readers old and new: Thank you for supporting me, especially during this new phase in my career. You all have been wonderful since my first book and it has been a blessing to have a fan base that has continued on with me through my journey. I truly appreciate you all!

To the reading groups: Thank you, thank you, thank you! You don't know how grateful I am to be a part of some of the best groups around and are so welcoming. I promise I'll name them all in my next book, but just know that you are not forgotten!

For everyone else who has helped me throughout my career (you know who you are), thank you so much. Just know that I appreciate everything that you have done and I really hope we all cross paths again someday.

Prologue: Morgan

March, 2008

"How much further do we have to go?"

I glanced at my friend Lamar and sighed. "This was your damn idea, so you better not bitch out on me now."

"Yeah, I gave the idea, I didn't think we would be going all over the city with a damn rug."

I stopped for a quick second to catch my breath before picking up the rug again and followed Lamar down the steep hill. I noticed an open field approaching which was a sight to behold because I didn't know how much longer I could continue walking and carrying this heavy ass shit.

"Honestly, I didn't know if we should do this. I said I would help you because of what happened, but…"

"You think this is something I wanted to do? Hell, this wasn't a part of my routine today, but it happened, so I had to figure out something so this wouldn't come back on me."

"I know, Morgan. I know what you went through and eventually this was going to happen. Just know that no matter what issues you have, whether it's outlandish as this, just know I got your back."

"I know and I appreciate it."

We got further down the hill and stopped near a shallow hole, which was perfect for what we needed to do. Lamar took off his backpack while I put the folded up rug on the ground.

"You got everything?"

"I got what I could get from the house." Lamar said as he took out two bottles of lighter fluid and a box of matches.

He gave me a bottle as he opened up his. I wondered should we take what was inside out of the rug, but figured I didn't need to see that again. I saw it enough earlier and that's something I didn't want to picture again.

We began pouring the fluid over the rug, making sure it was completely lathered. Lamar grabbed the box of matches and handed it to me.

"Care to do the honors."

I nodded as I took one out of the box and lighted it. I watched the flame go as I toss it onto the rug. It quickly spread, causing a huge inferno. Hopefully no one was around to see what was happening, but we chose this place carefully since no one really came to this park.

I threw another match onto the rug, making sure it burned to a fucking crisp. I didn't need any trace to what happened to be visible, so I would use the entire box if needed.

"I think we need to go Mo before someone sees the fire."

I continued to stare at the blaze wondering how things got to this point. One minute I was trying to live a normal life and the next I was in a park burning up evidence to something I'd done.

"Morgan, we need to go!"

I couldn't move as I just watch the one thing that has destroyed my life go up in flames. I should be upset or a little guilty for what happened, but honestly, I was fucking happy for what I was witnessing. I know I would have to live with this for the rest of my life, but at least I didn't have to deal with the bullshit anymore.

I did what I had to do to protect my mom and myself. If given the choice, I wouldn't hesitate in doing it again...

1. Morgan

"Are you seriously going to do this right now?"

"Do what? I told you before we came in here what my intentions were. You agreed to them, so I thought everything was straight."

The girl, Chelsea, Cecilia, whatever her name was, gave me an impatient glance before pulling down her skirt. I didn't know what her deal was, but I told her point blank what I wanted right now, and striking up a conversation wasn't one of them. I glanced at Carrie—that's her name – taking in her medium-length honey blonde hair, smooth auburn-colored skin, and knockout body that I wanted pressed up against me, but I guess she had other ideas. When I told her I wanted to have some fun, I thought she automatically knew what I meant. I thought wrong.

"Listen, if you think I'm just going to give it up to you right now, you're sadly mistaken."

"Hasn't stopped most girls before," I said with a sexy grin.

Carrie shook her head and sighed.

"I'm not one of these girls you're occasionally with on campus, I have more respect for myself than that."

"Maybe so, but I think you wanted to see for yourself what girls say about me."

"Get over yourself, Morgan," she told me, going to the door and opening it.

I sighed and put on my shirt. Oh well, it didn't matter. She wasn't the first girl and definitely wouldn't be the last. I knew I should stop being an ass towards women, but to be honest, I couldn't help it. I just wanted to have fun and not be tied down to anyone. I mean, was it a crime to feel that way? To my knowledge, it wasn't, so why should anyone else be upset about it? The only concern I had before graduating college was living my life, and if that included banging every female at Thompson University, then damn it, I would.

Maybe there was a reason why I felt this way. No, it didn't have anything to do with a relationship that went wrong or a girl cheating on me; it's just the fact that I hadn't met anyone worth committing to. Most of the girls I'd dated were just like me, only wanting to have fun and not be tied down. But, of course, I was the one looking like the man-whore. My mom thought so, and even my best friend, Lamar thought so. I never really understood why Lamar would think that when he was the same way. Well, he was until he met his current girlfriend, Tamara Morris. The two met during our sophomore year at Thompson, and she automatically turned Lamar into a whipping boy. Nothing was wrong with that, but it wasn't my style.

I walked over to the mirror near the dresser and looked at my reflection. There could be one girl who could make me change my ways, if I wanted to. Hayley Stevens. Hayley was the definition of perfection. Smooth, creamy skin the color of brown sugar, black natural curls that I wanted to twist my fingers through all day and night, and her lips. Full, thick lips that I wanted to suck and kiss on for eternity. Did I mention that girl had a banging body? Yes, she definitely did. I couldn't help but notice how her hips were shaped in her favorite jeans or her long legs walking past me when she wore her signature baby doll dresses. She oozed sexiness without even trying. She just naturally was.

I shook my head, trying to shake my thoughts of her. I opened the door and saw her and her friend, Paula Howard, walking towards the stairs. She looked at me with a confident smile and pushed her curls away from her face.

"Hey, Morgan,"

"Hey, Hayley. I didn't think you would be here."

"What, I can't be at a Kappa party?"

"Well, you know how Lamar is."

"Well, what Lamar doesn't know won't hurt him, right?" She asked, giving me a flirtatious smile.

I stared at her, thinking how sexy this girl was. I knew she was flirting with me, and being the man that I am, I could probably use it to my advantage, but I knew I couldn't. Not with her.

Paula looked at us and sighed.

"Let's go, Hales. Bye, Morgan," she said, pulling Hayley along as they went downstairs.

I exhaled and put a hand to my chest. Damn, I wanted her, but I knew if I pursued her, it would only cause trouble.

I could have any girl at Thompson University, and I almost did, but there was one girl I couldn't have, and that was Hayley. The reason? Hayley is my best friend's sister.

2. Hayley

I walked down the stairs, wondering when my heart would stop racing. With the way it was going, I thought it would jump out of my chest and leap onto the floor. I took slow, deep breaths to control my feelings. Paula looked at me then rolled her eyes at how I was carrying on.

"Hayley Bianca Stevens, can you get a grip?! In fact, why don't you just go back upstairs and kiss him or jump his bones or something? The constant flirting between you two is getting on my nerves."

"I would if I could, but you know I can't."

"Yeah, yeah. If Lamar found out about your attraction to his best friend, he would have you shipped off to Timbuktu and have Morgan swimming with the fishes. I've heard the story before, and honestly, it's kind of disturbing."

I accidentally bumped into someone on the way to the main hallway, causing the guy's drink to shift in his hand.

"Sorry," I quickly apologized before going to the living room of the Kappa Si Kappa fraternity house. Coming to their weekly party had been exciting at first, but now it was completely lame. Maybe the thrill was gone because I'd seen how fine Morgan looked upstairs. What I wouldn't do to go back upstairs, grab him and have my way with him.

Morgan Carter was the type of guy any woman would want to have a wet dream about, if that's possible. The guy was sexy! Smooth, ivory skin with a bit of a tan, clear blue eyes that I could look into all day and night, and short, dirty blonde hair I could run my fingers through. And his body! Hmm, the things I would do to it! His lean, athletic body had been featured in plenty of fantasies since I started liking boys. But it wasn't just his physical attributes that attracted me to him. To some, he was just a playboy, or a womanizer, but to me, he's just Morgan. When he would be around me, he would be the complete opposite. He was caring and sweet and a bit goofy. But that's what I liked about him. I just wished other people could see that. Well, mainly Lamar.

Since our parents divorced when I was six and Lamar was eight, he felt he had to be my protector. He always tried to be a father to me, when frankly, he never needed to be. It wasn't like our father passed away or anything. To be honest, our father was around the house more after the divorce compared to when our parents were together. It was kind of strange, but I guess that's a story for another time.

Growing up, Lamar took the role of big brother a little too far. He never really wanted me to have male friends, and he even tried to stop me from dating when I turned 16, but my parents quickly pulled in the reins. They probably didn't want me to date either, but they trusted me enough to be my own person; something Lamar couldn't do. I guess he still looked at me as his little sister, the girl who wore pigtails and carried her Cabbage Patch dolls wherever she went. Now, those days were long gone, and I was now a beautiful, young woman who was capable of making her own decisions. I just wished he would realize that.

I noticed Morgan walking over to us. He looked apologetic as he took Paula and my arms and pulled us to the door.

"What are you doing?" I asked angrily, trying to pull my arm from his grasp.

"You know I have to do this. If Lamar knew you were here and found out I knew about it, he would have both our asses."

"Are you always going to let Lamar have you by your balls? Damn, loosen up," Paula chided.

Morgan rolled his eyes at her, then he turned to me.

"Hales, you know I can't have you here."

"Why not? In case you haven't noticed, I'm 20 now, and I can pretty much figure things out on my own. I can't keep having you and Lamar on my back every day, dictating what I do. Bad enough I had to deal with his controlling ways at home, now I have to endure it at college, too."

"You know you could have gone to another college, right?" Paula interjected.

"Please, and have Lamar transfer schools?"

"You have a weird family," Paula said, shaking her head.

Morgan looked annoyed by us; he cleared his throat to get our attention.

"Excuse me, but you two have to go. In fact, why don't I just walk you back to the dorms? I'm heading out any way."

"You don't have to do that. We were leaving any way."

"What if I want to?" Morgan asked.

Paula smiled and slowly backed away.

"I think I'm going to stick around. I can get a ride with Shamicka if it gets too late."

I looked at Paula with a tiny smile.

"Maybe you should come with us too, Paula," Morgan suggested.

"I don't have a controlling brother, so I can stay," she said and went into the crowd.

I turned to Morgan, who ran a hand through his cropped hair.

"I guess we should go then," I said, walking in front of him.

Who knew leaving this party would be a great idea? Hopefully, things would go even better once Morgan and I were alone.

3. Morgan

Once we left the Kappa house, Hayley and I walked towards Hudson Hall, the junior co-ed dorms at Thompson. I looked over at Hayley, who turned towards me.

"You know, Paula made a point earlier."

"If you're referring to Lamar having my balls, then you're both wrong. I can do whatever I want. You know that."

"I do, but when it comes to me, you don't."

I looked at Hayley, wondering where this boldness was coming from. It shouldn't really surprise me though; the girl had always been fiery, especially towards her brother. She would state her case on various arguments until she had the last word. To me, that was kind of a turn on.

I stopped walking as I turned my body towards her. I stared into her brown eyes, pushing a strand of hair from her face.

"Hales, you're like my little sister. We've known each other since we were in elementary school. I just feel maybe we shouldn't cross that line."

"Cross what line? Morgan, I see the way you look at me, and trust me, it's not a stare siblings would give to each other."

I stared at her, our bodies close together, her eyes gazing into mine. I was trying my hardest to not give into this girl, but everything in me wanted to go into her dorm room and just let everything go. But I couldn't do it.

Lamar and I had been best friends since we were five. I had just moved into town, so of course I didn't have any friends. On my first day of kindergarten, my mom urged me to take my Transformers to school, hoping that maybe it would be a way for someone to talk to me. For some reason, my mom thought I had a hard time making friends. Who wouldn't at five years old? Anyway, during recess, Lamar approached me, noticing them and automatically started a conversation about them. Before I knew it, we were running around the playground pretending we were Optimus Prime and Bumblebee.

After that, the two of us became good friends. We hung out at each other's houses, had sleepovers, and even went on family vacations together. I became a part of Lamar's family, just like he did with mine. As time went by, it became clear that not only were we good friends, but we were like brothers. It was something I always wanted, because I was the only child. We leaned on each other for a lot of things, from Lamar's parents and their divorce, to the numerous girls we encountered, we developed a brotherly bond that was unbreakable.

With Hayley, at first I did just look at her as Lamar's sister. She always had those dolls with her and wanted to hang out with us as we played basketball or just talked. But as time passed, I did noticed how much she changed. I tried not to, but I couldn't help it. I know Lamar wouldn't want me with her, mainly because of my history with women, but honestly, he wouldn't want any man to be around Hayley, because that was his sister, plain and simple.

"You know how much your family means to me. You all helped me feel welcome when I first moved to Mission Glen. That's something I will always remember."

"What does that have to do with us? If you think you have feelings for me, why fight them?"

"You know why?"

"I get it; you would think that we're betraying Lamar if we do, but Morgan, don't you think you should go for what you want?"

"We need to go." I said as I started back walking.

Hayley stopped me, grabbing my arm and pulling me towards her. She put her arms around me, giving me a sensual glance.

"I never expected you to act like this. Around campus, you break all the rules. You're straightforward with everyone you encounter, but the one person you should be honest with, you don't."

"Because I know if I do, it will lead to disaster."

"But wouldn't you want to know how things would be between us?" Hayley asked, pressing her body against me.

I breathed heavily against her, putting my hand across her shoulder, feeling how soft her skin felt beside mine.

"Every single day,"

"Well, why won't you let go? Just one night, just see what it's like. No thoughts, no worries. Just you and me, together," she said.

I leaned into her even further, taking in the mango scent in her hair, her fingertips gliding across my shoulders. At that point, I was completely horny. I grabbed her hand, sliding it down my stomach. She continued to stare at me as I pressed her palm against the hardness of my jeans. Her breathing became erratic while her hand moved against me.

"That's how bad I want you, but it's not going to happen." I said.

I let go of her hand, disconnecting us from the reaction.

"Come on." I said, walking towards the dorm entrance.

I heard Hayley give a soft moan as she walked behind me. I needed to hurry up and get her inside so I could go back to my apartment. I didn't think I could take another minute alone with her, because I would end up doing something that would destroy the only real friendship I ever had.

We finally approached the door, as Hayley pulled out her entrance card to grant access. She looked at me, giving me an apologetic smile.

"Morgan..."

"It's okay. You don't have to apologize."

"I can go in from here."

"No, I'll walk you to your room."

"You don't have to."

"I want to."

Hayley sighed as she led the way to her dorm room. While walking, I had to wonder how she was able to stay in a co-ed dorm. I'm sure Lamar had something to say about it, but knowing Hayley, she did something to get her request fulfilled.

Once we reached her doorstep, she paused to stare at me one more time.

"Morgan, if things weren't so complicated, would we really have given into the attraction we have towards each other?"

I stared at her, a smile going across my lips.

"No, I wouldn't have."

Hayley gave a disappointed pout to what I just said.

"Hales, you deserve much more than a one-night stand, so, no I wouldn't have just given into my attraction for you. Instead, I would have given us a chance for something more." I said.

I went up to her, slightly pressing my lips against her cheek. Before I knew it, she turned her lips towards mine, kissing me. Damn, her lips felt so good! She pulled me closer to her, wrapping her arms around me. I put my hands through her hair, touching those curls I imagined doing every day for years. I wanted to resist kissing her, but I couldn't anymore. I wanted to feel her lips against mine, her tongue moving with mine. I needed this. I needed her.

She quickly released herself from me, putting her key into the lock. I leaned into her, pushing her hair to the side, kissing her neck. She softly moaned, managing to unlock the door. She turned around, bringing me inside and slammed the door.

We moved towards the wall. Her back pressed against it while I held her closer to me. Her hands were underneath my shirt, trying to lift it off my body. I was doing the same to her, lightly touching her soft skin, kissing her neck and chest. She pulled my shirt off, staring at my chest. She smiled, moving her lips down my body. A moan quickly flew out of my mouth, leading me to take her towards her bed.

We lay down, stopping to stare at each other. I knew I shouldn't partake in this. To give into my weakness for her. I made a promise to myself and to Lamar that I would never try to pursue Hayley. That was a vow I gave to my best friend and mainly to myself, because I knew I would hurt her. If we ever got together, I would find some way to screw it up. I need to end this now before I got too involved.

I got up, going over to the floor to pick up my shirt. Hayley sat up on the bed, completely confused as to what was going on.

"What's wrong?"

"I'm not going to do this."

"Why not?"

"You know why. With the way things are, it's best if we remain friends."

Hayley sighed as she walked over to me.

"I don't understand you. You'd rather be with these other females around campus, but you don't want to take a chance on something real. Something that will last more than one night."

I put my shirt on, trying really hard not to take her back into my arms and do all the things I've dreamt about doing to her. I turned towards her, putting my arms around her. I kissed her, taking my time with her, because I knew this would be the last time I could be like this with her.

My hands roamed down to her body, getting a chance to feel her skin. I touched the small of her back. My hands went lower to her ass, wishing I didn't go there, because now I was hard again. Hayley put her hands through my hair, caressing my lips with hers.

"Let me leave you with something so you'll always remember this moment," she said.

She pulled me back to the bed and before I knew it, it was over. I couldn't fight my feelings for her. I knew I would regret it, but right now, the only thing I wanted was to be with her; and now, I was going to get my chance to.

4. Hayley

I slowly opened my eyes and quickly closed them. The morning sun was in my face, which I really didn't appreciate. I was not a morning person and today was no exception.

I rolled over on my side, expecting Morgan to still be beside me, but to my surprise, he wasn't there. I raised up and looked around the room. Not only wasn't he in the bed, but his clothes were gone.

I lay down and sighed. I really thought we had a breakthrough last night. He finally let go of his hesitation with me which was something I'd been waiting on for years. Don't get me wrong, I wasn't sitting around waiting for the moment that Morgan finally noticed me. I did my own thing with dating other guys. I had fun with them, but they weren't him. I constantly compared them to him and it was starting to get in the way of me dating.

All of a sudden, a loud bang was escalating outside my door. I jumped up, wondering what the hell was that, when Paula's loud ass voice vibrated from the other end.

"I know you're here, Hales! Open up!"

I quickly got out of bed and ran to the door. I didn't need the RA to come to my room about Paula being loud. Theresa already said if she did it again, she was not allowed back on the floor.

"Do you really need to act like this so early in the morning?"

"What? I was trying to wake you up. Consider me your alarm clock."

I rolled my eyes and opened the door wider for her to come in. She started to look around, and went under the bed. I stared at her with a curious glance.

"What are you doing?"

"I'm checking to see if Morgan left anything behind. I know you two got some last night."

"And how would you know? He just dropped me off, that's all."

"Please, Hales. I could tell the way you two were looking when you left that you were going to have sex."

I sighed and went to the bed and sat down. "He could have at least stayed, but that's Morgan for you. He only cares about himself."

"Stop, Paula!"

"Stop what? Morgan is a player. In the short time that I've known him, his ultimate goal is to get into every female's drawers. Hell, I'm surprised he hasn't tried to get into mines, which I would never give up anyway."

"Are you done?"

"No, I'm not. You deserve so much more, Hales. You probably think in the back of your mind that you could change his bad boy ways, but honestly, you can't. He smooth-talked you into fucking him and it worked. Now, where is he? Let me guess, probably moved on to his next conquest."

"He's not like that."

"If you say so. Anyway, this is just a lesson learned. Now, you've did what you wanted with him and it's out of your system, so you can move on."

"Maybe so." I said to myself.

"I have to ask though, how was he? I mean, I heard so much about white guys..."

"I'm not going to tell you that, Paula."

"Why not? We're girls; we tell each other everything."

"Well, unfortunately, not this. Can we just move on to another topic? Why are you really here?"

"I was hoping I could invite you out for breakfast. I was going to meet up with Scott and Brandon at the coffeehouse."

"I don't think so."

"Come on; I thought you would be glad to see Brandon, especially with everything that has happened between you and Morgan."

I shook my head and sighed. Brandon and I had been dating for a little while now. Basically, he was my distraction from Morgan. From his mixed blue-green eyes to his honey-colored skin and his fit body, he was definitely easy to look at. Not only that, but he was easy to get along with. He was definitely boyfriend material, but there was something about him that made me wonder if he was too good to be true.

"I have a lot of studying to do."

"Really, Hayley? You can take an hour out for breakfast."

"Paula, I don't..."

"Be ready in 5. I'll be waiting." She said. She patted the top of my head and went to the door.

I watched it close and flopped down on the bed. I really didn't want to go out and be social. The night I had with Morgan was amazing, which was definitely making me feel a little upset with what he'd done. I knew he would do this, but I took a chance with him anyway. Now, I definitely regretted being with him.

***

After showering and getting into a peach bulky sweater and grey skinny jeans, I met up with Paula outside. I put my hair into a hat, wishing I had more time to tame it, but it didn't matter anyway. It's not like I was going to impress anyone right now.

We approached the coffeehouse in five minutes and saw Brandon and Scott sitting at a booth near the window. Paula immediately went to Scott and gave him a sensual kiss. Scott was Paula's man for the moment, which I used that term loosely. Paula is sort of the female version of Morgan, so it kind of surprised me that she would talk about Morgan when she does the same thing.

"How are you this morning, pretty lady?" Brandon asked and smiled.

I looked at him and gave a shy smile. "I'm doing great. How about yourself?"

"Pretty damn good since I see you."

I blushed, completely smitten by the way he was being with me. I had to admit, now that I knew where things stood with Morgan, I probably could actually give Brandon a chance.

"I was thinking if you're not too busy with studying that we could go into the city this week? Maybe grab some dinner and see a movie."

I smiled. "Sure, that would be great."

"And Lamar won't have a problem with that, will he?"

"At this point, I could care less about my brother." I said.

He leaned into me and gave me a kiss that literally made me wet. I didn't know what was going on with me, but I guess my little obsession with Morgan was quickly fading away.

Once I pulled away from Brandon, I could see him and Lamar walking in. I stared at him as he gave me a quick glance before going to the counter. Paula looked at me and over at Morgan and sighed.

My phone beeped as I dug into my cross body bag. I looked at the text from Paula reading: "His lost, Hales,"

I nodded as Brandon put an arm around me. I snuggled against him and closed my eyes. Paula's right. If he didn't realize the person that I was, then the hell with him.

5. Morgan

I glanced over at Hayley talking to that punk assed Brandon. I couldn't stand him. He thought he could get with any woman because of those damn eyes. I bet they wouldn't be any good once I punched them out of his sockets.

"Morgan!"

I looked over and saw Lamar giving me an intense look. Damn, I hope he didn't see who I was staring at.

"What?"

"Did you want anything?"

"Nah, I'm good."

"What is your problem? You've been out of it since you came in this morning, which you still haven't said where you were all night."

I sighed and ran a hand through my hair. Like I would tell him I was banging his sister the entire night. Damn, I still couldn't believe that happened between Hayley and me. The way she felt was incredible. I wanted so bad to stay with her and be with her, but we both knew that could never happen.

Once Lamar got his order he went straight over to Hayley's table. I gave the side eye, wondering if I should even walk over there, but Hayley saw me staring at her, so I didn't have a choice.

"So, I see you're hanging out instead of studying."

"So nice to see you too, Lamar. I'm doing great, by the way." Hayley retorted with a sly smile.

"Don't start, Hales."

"Start what? Honestly, I didn't think I would be going to college with my dad, but I guess I am with how you're talking to me."

Lamar rolled his eyes while I grinned.

"Someone has to watch over you."

"Lamar, how many times do I need to tell you that I can take care of myself? I don't need you to protect me."

"Maybe not now, but eventually, you will."

"Trust me, Lamar, Hales is in good hands." Brandon said as he snuggled closer to her. I wanted so bad to chop that damn arm off of him.

Hayley looked at me. She quickly looked away and got up from the booth.

"I'll be back." She said to everyone. She went in the direction of the restrooms, which gave me an idea. Paula stared at me and shook her head, but I didn't care.

"I'm going to the restroom." I told Lamar and went behind Hayley.

As soon as she was going around the corner, I grabbed her and pulled her back to the wall. She stared directly into my eyes with a displeased look.

"What do you want, Morgan?"

"I needed to talk to you."

"About what? You made it clear this morning when you left without saying anything."

"You know I had to, just in case Lamar came by."

"Stop it! I'm tired of you using my brother as an excuse. Just admit that you only wanted to sleep with me. Well, you got your damn wish."

"You know that's not true. Hayley, I do care about you and hurting you is not something I wanted to do."

"Really, well you're doing a damn good job of it."

"You think I want to do that when all I want to do right now is kiss those sexy lips of yours. How much I want to take you back to my place, undress you and make your body cum over and over again until I have you begging me to stop."

Her eyes gazed over my body as I grabbed her waist. I pinned her against the wall and kissed her. She tried to resist me, but she didn't stand a chance. She wanted me just as much as I wanted her. After last night, I didn't know how much longer I could stay away from her. If I had my wish, I wouldn't let her out of my sight.

She pulled me closer to her as I leaned my body against hers. She stopped kissing me and stared into my eyes.

"What are we really doing? We danced around our feelings for years and we finally gave in last night. What would make me believe that we'll go back to where we started?"

"If you're referring to this morning, just know that I didn't want to leave you."

"You didn't have to. You had a choice and you made it by walking out. I don't know if I want to keep playing by your rules. Don't expect me to sit around and wait for you, because I'm not."

"I don't want you to, but I want to make you see that I really do care about you; I just wish things could have been different."

Hayley shook her head. "It can be, if you just try hard enough."

She pushed past me and walked back to the lounge. I cursed under my breath and punched the wall. I was trying my hardest to make her see that I could be who she wanted me to be. After last night, I would do everything in my power to make her change her mind; even if it did cost me my friendship with Lamar.

6. Hayley

After that awkward moment with Morgan, I went straight to the table and told everyone I had a headache and left. I needed to get away from there as quickly as possible, so I ended back in my room.

I stared at the wall, trying to contemplate on what to do. I really wanted to call my mom. Besides Paula, my mom also knew I had a crush on Morgan. She figured it out one day when I was nine and was following him and Lamar around the backyard. She thought it was cute and told me maybe things could change when we both became older. Boy, was she wrong.

I looked at my phone, wondering if I should call her, when I saw a text from Morgan. I rolled my eyes and threw it on the bed. I was not going to talk to him. Although, I wanted for us to find some leeway for a potential relationship, I knew I couldn't. He made his decision when he left my room earlier.

The two of us had shared some close moments together, but last night really showed that there could have been something between us. Maybe he was right; we shouldn't have tried to pursue anything. Honestly, I didn't know why I would want to if he was being this way. If he couldn't stand up to my brother and declare his feelings for me, then he wasn't someone I should be with. Plain and simple.

There was a knock at the door and I went to it. I opened it and saw Lamar's girlfriend, Tamara, on the other end. Ever since the two of them has been together, she has become a really great friend to me. While Paula was more of the free-spirited friend, Tamara was the reasonable one. I was always able to get good advice from her, whether I wanted to hear it or not.

"Hey, come on in." I said as I opened the door wider.

"Thanks. Lamar said you wasn't feeling well, so I brought over some notes for psych."

I looked at the clock on my nightstand and sighed. I didn't even know I missed my class. Shit!

"Thanks. I must have been out of it."

"I guess so. How are you feeling?"

"Better, now; thanks."

"This doesn't have anything to do with a certain guy, does it?"

I looked at her while she gave a smirk.

"I don't know what you're talking about?"

"Oh please, I know when it's about a guy. So spill, is Brandon giving you a hard time about something? Or is it that stubborn Lamar? I told him to leave you two alone."

I gave a sigh of relief when she said Brandon. If she knew about Morgan, she would definitely run and tell Lamar. Those two didn't keep anything from each other.

"Everything's cool, Tam."

"Really? I could talk to Lamar again."

"You don't have to. In fact, we're planning on going out later this week."

"Hopefully it's not tonight. Some girls from the sorority and I were going to hit Onyx and I wanted to see if you wanted to come with."

"I don't know. I have a lot of studying to do."

"Oh, well I don't want to keep you from it."

"That doesn't mean I wasn't going."

Tamara smiled. "Okay, well we're leaving at 9, so we could swing by here if you want."

"No, I can meet you all there. I'll probably bring Paula though."

"That's fine, but you're taking care of her if she gets sloppy drunk."

"Don't I always?"

Tamara smiled and went to the door. "And you don't have to worry about Lamar. He's going out with the guys tonight."

"When do I ever think about Lamar?"

"I know you don't, but it was a reminder."

I nodded and Tamara left the room.

I went back to the bed and lay down. I really did need to study, but I also needed to take my mind off of Morgan by going out and having some fun.

***

After getting a few hours of sleep, I was able to start getting ready for tonight. I looked at myself in the full-length mirror, wondering if the black and grey printed minidress was the perfect outfit. I was going to try on another one, but decided I didn't need to. I wanted to feel sexy tonight and this dress was definitely doing it for me.

I worked my hair into a nice twist, but decided to take it down. I loved how my hair looked when it was free.

I looked at my reflection and thought about the other night with Morgan. His kisses set my entire body on fire. The way he was with me was a little rough, but gentle at the same time. It was as if he didn't know whether to be one way or the other with me; as if he didn't want to hurt me.

I knew then that his feelings for me were a little different from the other girls he's dated. I knew he wanted to change and in some way, he was willing to; but with his loyalty to my brother, it wasn't going to happen anytime soon. For years those two has been involved in some sort of pact that made Morgan stay clear of me. I don't know what it was that Lamar had over him, but it had to be big. One thing I know about Morgan Carter is that he didn't give a shit about anything and anyone; so whatever it was, it was destroying any chance of us being together.

I looked at myself one last time before grabbing my car keys and clutch. I told Paula I would be at her room by 8:45. Hopefully she was ready to head out.

7. Morgan

I glanced at my reflection and sighed. I really didn't want to go out tonight, but since Maurice had just dumped his girlfriend today, he felt he should have celebrated by going out. Honestly, I thought he would have taken it hard since he found her cheating with his brother, but he was taking it better than I thought. He even invited his brother along with us, but he declined, thinking he probably was going to beat his ass later. Really, after a few drinks in him, he just might have.

One good thing about tonight was that Lamar wouldn't be with us. He was going out with his frat brothers to a concert, so at least I didn't have to put up a front for him. Since last night, I couldn't even look at him in the face without thinking about Hayley. Once he found out about us, he would be pissed and probably try and kill me, but at this point, I didn't care. I really wanted to be with her, but now, I had to show to her that I really wanted to. I let her down when leaving her earlier in the day; so now, I really have to mean it if I wanted to go all out for her.

I put on my brown leather jacket over my black T-shirt and looked at myself again. I looked good. Hopefully tonight, I could try and have some fun.

Once Maurice and our other friend, Caleb arrived at my apartment, we headed to Onyx. Caleb was already drunk as he stuck his head out of the window, whistling at every female that walked past the car. Couldn't take his ass anywhere. While Lamar was the serious one, Maurice and Caleb were the fun ones. They would make you forget about your problems in an instant. So no matter what I was going through right now, I knew I would have a decent time with those two.

"Damn, who is that?" Caleb asked while looking ahead.

I looked in the same direction as Caleb and took in the black and grey minidress. Even though her back was turned from us, I knew that body from anywhere. Her hair was a dead giveaway as she pushed some from the side of her face.

"Shit, that's Hayley. Good thing Lamar isn't here; he probably would have killed my ass." Caleb said while laughing.

"I don't understand what Lamar's deal is? Hayley is fine as shit." Maurice added.

"If you think so, then why you haven't stepped to her?" Caleb asked.

"Because I was with Shannon, which was a damn mistake. Next time, if I mention anything about online dating, just deck me."

"I told you about getting with someone from a dating site." Caleb said.

I looked at the two then back at Hayley. She finally turned around and saw me staring at her. Our eyes locked as she slowly licked her lips. She gave a sexy smile as she went inside with Paula and Tamara.

"What was that?" Maurice asked.

"What was what?"

"That exchange you two did? Her licking her lips at you. Is it something you need to tell us?"

"No, nothing at all." I replied.

We went inside and the latest from T.I. was bumping on the speakers throughout the club. The first thing I needed was a drink, so I headed straight to the bar. Once I ordered a beer, Hayley approached me and ordered a vodka cranberry.

"Shouldn't you be drinking a soda?" I asked.

"Shouldn't you be minding your own business?" She retorted and looked ahead.

"What was that outside?"

"What was what? I just thought you might have wanted something to think about on your way home to your lonely apartment later. Or for all I know, you'll probably be getting some sleaze to take home with you. Just know she would never be me." She said with a sly grin.

She was right about that.

"Hayley..."

"Like I said earlier, you made your choice, so just deal with it. Enjoy your night." She said as the bartender handed her drink.

Before I could say anything else, she walked off into the crowd.

I looked ahead at my beer and quickly drank it. I knew I shouldn't be drinking. I usually didn't because of my past; but tonight, I needed something to calm my nerves before I did something wreck less.

I ordered another one and went to find an empty table. I saw Caleb and Maurice already on the dance floor with two random chicks. I sat down and looked around, spotting Hayley near the center, dancing with Tamara. Damn, she looked sexy. I was enjoying the view when Paula quickly blocked it by sitting in front of me.

"She looks good, doesn't she?"

"Why are you sitting here? Shouldn't you be looking for your next victim to date?"

"Ha, ha, real funny Carter. If you didn't know, I'm very happy with the guy I'm with, thank you very much."

"If you say so."

"Listen, I know what happened between you and Hales and I have to say you should stay away from her."

I gave her a blank stare and continued drinking my beer.

"I know you hear me, Morgan."

"I heard you loud and clear. In fact, even with the music blazing everyone heard you with your loud ass."

"Don't play with me, Morgan! Hales is my best friend and I do not want to see her hurt. Just thinking about what happened goes to show that you can't handle a relationship with her, so just move along and find another girl to screw and let Hayley be with someone stable, like Brandon."

"Please, he can't do anything for her."

"He can be a great boyfriend for her, unlike you. I know you have baggage and Hayley doesn't need that in her life. She has a bright future ahead of her and she doesn't need someone like you bringing her down."

"What the fuck are you talking about? As you can see, I'm in college like you trying to further myself, so don't come at me like I'm not doing anything with my life."

She rolled her eyes at me and sighed.

"If I didn't know any better, you're probably jealous because I never made a pass at you; isn't it, Paula? You probably wondered why I never tried to get with you; just admit it."

"You're full of yourself."

"And you wished I wanted to fuck you."

She jumped up from the table and tried to grab my drink to throw at me, but I was too quick.

"You're a fucking pig."

"And I'm speaking the truth about you. In my opinion, Hayley deserves a better friend than you."

She turned around and walked onto the dance floor.

I laughed and drank the rest of my beer. That'll get her to leave me alone.

I continued to watch the dance floor when my phone started to vibrate. I dug into my pocket and looked at the name flashing across the screen. I sighed and put it back into my pocket. I knew I should answer it, since it was my mom, but I couldn't. Not right now. That's the third time she'd called today. Normally, she only called once a week, but I knew when she did multiple callings; it was only to talk about what happened.

That's a part of my life that I didn't want to relive. I had to move past that and actually be happy. I couldn't have a constant reminder of that night and the consequences it has caused me. I guess that's why I was the person I am today. I tried to block it out anyway I could, even if it was being with multiple women.

The sudden mood change made me get up and head back to the bar. I needed another drink.

***

After an hour later and three beers in me, it was time to head out. I wasn't feeling the atmosphere as I glanced at Maurice and Caleb still dancing with the same girls from earlier. Now I wished I had driven my car. Since they were my ride here, I couldn't leave.

I sat at the same table, when a girl came over wanting to dance with me. I waved my hand away and the girl pouted and stormed off.

"Whatever." I mumbled. That was the fourth girl who came up to me. Normally, I would have probably danced with one of them and tried to fuck her in the bathroom, but I wasn't trying to go there tonight. The only thing I wanted to do was finish out this night so I could go back to my place and crash.

I was checking my phone when I heard someone shouting and glanced over to the center of the dance floor. I saw the huge crowd surrounding something that was going on. I got up and went over to the scene with a curious glance. I stopped and saw what was happening. I saw Hayley dancing on some dude. Her dress was hiked up to her waist. She was slowly grinding on him as if she was having sex with him.

I glanced at the scene and shook my head. Why would she do this to herself? Evidently, she was drunk.

I pushed my way through the crowd and went over to her. I picked her up and put her over my shoulder when the crowd started booing.

"Put me down!" She yelled as she started hitting my back.

I ignored her as I continued out to the door. I didn't know where the hell Tamara or Paula was, but they should have been keeping an eye on her, especially since she was drunk.

I went over to the parking lot and to her car. I still had her over my shoulder when I realized she didn't have her keys.

"Shit." I said.

"Ha, can't find my keys, huh."

"Does someone have your things, Hales?"

"No, they're in my bra, so you're going to have to search me." She said and giggled.

I sighed and put her on her feet. I leaned her against the car, wondering if I wanted to do this.

"Come on, you know you want to." She said. Her eyes were daring me to as she took her hand into mine. She put it towards her chest, going down until she reached to her waist. She tried to go further, but I stopped her.

"Let's not go there."

"I never knew you to be so scary." She said.

I put her hand up to her chest so she could fish out her keys. If I had done it, I probably would be feeling a lot more than her breasts.

I guided her hand until I felt them. I pulled them out, opened the door and gently put her in the passenger seat. I saw her entrance card in the small compartment near the console. At least I didn't have to go in her bra again.

"I'm taking you to the dorm so you can sleep it off."

"No, I want to go back to your place."

"No, Hayley."

"Why not? Trust me, I'll make it worth your while. You fucked me so good last night that I had to touch myself earlier. In fact, I need you to fuck me again;

right here, right now." She said. She was struggling to take off her dress, hitting herself on the side of the door.

"Stop it, Hayley."

"Stop what? This is what you wanted, right? Sex with no strings attached. I'm willing to give that to you. Just enjoy the moment with me. No one has to know." She said as she kissed my neck.

I closed my eyes and sighed. I had to stop this.

"Hayley, you're drunk. I'm not going to have sex with you."

"I bet if I was some hoe off the street you would."

I started the ignition and pulled out of the parking lot. I needed to get her to her room and put her to bed.

Throughout the drive, I took a peek at her, in which she was fast asleep. I sighed, knowing I would have to carry her to her room. Hopefully no one, especially her brother, saw her like this.

When I arrived to the parking lot, I found her phone underneath the driver's side. I noticed the texts from Paula and Tamara, wondering where she was. I sent them one back, letting them know she was with me and back at her dorm.

I went over to her side and opened the door. I carried her in my arms and locked the door. After going up the floor and opening the door, I led her to the bed, gently putting her down. I slowly took off her shoes, trying not to wake her when she opened her eyes. She didn't say a word as I was able to get the left one off and was working to get the right one.

"Morgan..."

"Don't worry about it." I said.

I grabbed a blue and white striped blanket from the bed, which from my understanding was her favorite blanket. From what Lamar told me, their grandmother gave it to her when she was younger. I put it around her as she began snoring softly. I grabbed the trash can by her desk and put it near the bed in case she needed it. I went to the arm chair near the dresser and sat down, staring at her as she slept.

I knew I should go, but I didn't want to. I wasn't going to leave like I did the other night. Instead, I needed to see if she'll be okay later.

8. Hayley

I slowly opened my eyes and noticed the sun was peeking through the thin sheet I used as a curtain. I looked down, noticing I was completely naked. I glanced up and saw Morgan in the armchair, fully clothed and asleep.

What happened last night? I thought as I looked around the room.

I pulled my blanket even closer to me as a huge headache went through my temples. The only thing I remembered was drinking a continuous amount of vodka cranberries and dancing on some strange guy. The rest was a blur.

I still looked down, wondering why I was naked. Did Morgan and I have sex again? If so, why was he fully dressed?

"I see you're finally awake." Morgan said.

I gave him a surprised look. I needed to know why I was naked. Before I could say anything, he beat me to it.

"You threw up on your dress, so I had to take it off of you."

"You couldn't find any clothes for me to wear?"

"You were passed out Hales; so I put you back into the bed."

I sighed. "About last night..."

Morgan shook his head. "Don't. I've been there, so you don't have to explain. Where were Tamara and Paula, though?"

"I kind of ditched them and went off to do my own thing. I guess I shouldn't have done that, huh?"

"No, you shouldn't have. Anything could have happened to you if I didn't see you dancing on that guy."

"Which I probably shouldn't have been doing either."

"Well, lesson learned, right."

"I guess so. Why did you stay?"

"I needed to make sure you were okay."

We stared at each other when Morgan got up and went to the mini-fridge. That thing had been a life-saver for me since the dining hall served nothing but horrible food. The last time I'd eaten there was freshmen year.

"I went to the bakery and got you those muffins you like. I figured you would want them."

"Thanks, but I don't think I can eat anything."

"You probably should to cure your hangover."

I smiled as he handed the bag to me.

"So, what led you to get sloppy drunk last night?"

I sighed and opened the bag. I really didn't want to get into this with him.

"Was it because of me?"

"Don't flatter yourself, Carter."

"I'm being serious Hales. You're not a heavy drinker, so something must have been on your mind."

Before I could answer, Morgan's phone started to ring. He picked it up from the desk and glanced at it while giving a frustrated sigh. He put it back down and looked at me.

"Are you going to answer that?"

"No."

"Why not?"

"Because I'm not. Just answer the question, Hales."

"Not until you tell me why you don't want to answer your phone. Is it one of your groupies stalking you?"

"It's my mom."

I raised my eyebrow, wondering why he didn't want to talk to her.

"Is everything okay between you two?"

"Couldn't be better."

"Why are you upset that she was calling you?"

"I don't want to talk about it, so just drop it."

I stared at him and tossed the bag on the bed.

"I'm sorry, I shouldn't have snapped at you."

"It's cool; you're not obligated to say anything to me, just like I'm not with why I was drinking last night. But if you must know, I needed to not think for a second and actually have fun. I wanted to know what it felt like not to have to be on guard all of the time, especially when Lamar is around."

He sighed. "I understand how you feel."

We continued to stare at each other when he walked over to me. I knew he could hear my heart beating as he sat down beside me. He gently grabbed my hand and pulled me over to him, giving me a kiss that made me forget everything, including my damn name.

He pulled the blanket from me and slowly caressed my breast, quickly causing them to become hard from his touch. I began to pant while his lips moved down my neck, tasting my skin. He felt so good. Him being anywhere near my body felt like ecstasy to me.

He was about to lay me down on the bed when a loud bang came from outside.

"Open up, Hayley!"

We both looked at each other, knowing what that meant.

"You have to hide."

"What?! I'm not hiding."

"Do you really want Lamar to see you here? Just go in the closet."

"I can't fit in the closet."

"You're going to have to try today."

I jumped up and pushed Morgan off of the bed. I shoved him into the closet and shut the door. I went to my dresser and grabbed what I could find to wear.

"Hayley Stevens, open this damn door, now!"

I took a deep breath and went to the door. I opened it and gave Lamar a bright smile. My smile quickly faded when I saw Brandon standing beside him.

"Good morning, you two."

"Don't give me that! I can't believe you. How could you get drunk and make an ass out of yourself at the club last night?"

I tilted my head, wondering how in the hell he knew that. Even Tamara and Paula wouldn't have known that since I ditched them to go dance.

"How did you know?"

"One of my friends saw you at Onyx last night. And where the hell is Morgan? They said he was the one who took you out of the building."

"Why would I know where Morgan is? I just woke up and as you can see, I'm the only one here."

Lamar folded his arms across his chest while Brandon gave me a doubtful expression. Based on that look, I didn't know what Brandon was implying. Honestly, I didn't even know why he was here.

"And when have you and Brandon become friends?" I asked, trying to change the subject.

"Don't change the subject. He was at the door when I arrived anyway."

"Listen, as many times as I have said it, I'm not a little girl anymore. If I want to drink, then I will."

"I don't know how when you're underage. Who in the hell bought you drinks?"

"Like I would tell you,"

He went over to my clutch and started dumping everything out. I went over to him, trying to stop him from going through my things. Had he lost his damn mind?

"Where is it?"

"What?!"

"Don't play dumb with me! Where is your fake ID.?"

"I don't have one. Now, get away from my stuff!" I yelled.

Good thing my ID was in the car where I'm sure Morgan had left it. I didn't need any more issues to occur between me and my overbearing brother.

"Yo, Lamar, chill." Brandon said.

"Was I even saying anything to you?" He said while staring at him.

Brandon held his hands up and went over to the dresser. I watched him as he looked down. I closed my eyes, hoping he didn't see Morgan's phone. I remembered he set it by the desk and he didn't take it with him in the closet. I gave a silent prayer as he continued to look. He stared at me with a sly grin.

"Whose phone is this, Hales?"

My heart started pounding, as he held up Morgan's phone.

"It looks like Morgan's." Lamar said.

"No; it's actually mines. I just brought a new case, so it's probably similar to his." I quickly replied.

I went over to him and snatched the phone from his hand and put it on my nightstand.

Brandon gave me a curious look before coming over to me. He gave me a kiss on the cheek, which made Lamar's temples flare.

"I'll let you talk with your brother. Call me when you have some free time."

"Sure." I said, knowing good well I wasn't.

He walked out of the door and Lamar slammed it.

"Don't slam my damn door! You know how people are on this floor."

"Stop it, Hayley! Since the time you have been here you have done nothing but rebel against me. Is it because of Mom and Dad and the divorce?"

I shook my head and laughed. "Are you that damn delusional? It's because of you and your wannabe dad routine. Even he doesn't act like this towards me."

"Hayley..."

"Stop! In fact, you need to leave."

"Not until we talk."

"I don't want to talk to you, Lamar. Just give me some time to think."

He sighed and rubbed his hand over his low-cut fade. He went to the door and opened it.

He turned around to stare at me. "Just know that everything I do, it's to protect you, sis. Don't ever forget that."

He closed the door and I quickly went to lock it. Morgan walked out of the closet and came over to me. He pulled me into his arms and hugged me.

"I was seconds from coming out and decking your brother."

"Morgan, don't."

"No; he had no right talking to you like that."

I began to shake as he held me tighter. "Brandon spotted your phone."

"I don't care. If he comes after me, then I'll be ready for him."

"You know he won't."

"Trust me, he will."

"What are we going to do now?"

Morgan pulled away from me and smiled. "I'm willing to fight for you, if that's what you're implying."

I smiled. "Really?"

"Yeah. You're worth fighting for."

I smiled as he kissed me. I never knew Morgan Carter would say those words about me. Now, I just hope he could live up to them, because he was definitely going to be in for one.

9. Morgan

Since I decided to be with Hayley, I needed clever ways to actually see her. Even though I came to the point that I didn't care about Lamar finding out, I didn't want to add any more issues to Hayley, so we would keep things a secret for now.

After leaving her room, I went back to the apartment and Lamar laid out the questions for me. I quickly answered them and went into my room, not giving anything away to where I was or what I was doing.

Throughout the day, I decided I wanted to do something nice for Hales by planning our first date. I knew she was a laid-back type of girl, so she wouldn't want anything fancy; but I wanted it to be memorable. I was willing to pull out my most prized possession, which she has been begging me to do for years. Now, she was going to have her chance tonight.

After lounging around the apartment for a few hours, I was back at her room. I lightly knocked on the door, knowing how her floor mates were. She opened it and smiled.

"Hey. What are you doing here?"

"Damn, you're already tired of me?"

"You know I'm not; I'm just surprised you're back."

"Well, I said I was willing to go all in with you, so now, I am. In fact, get ready because I'm taking you out."

"Really?"

"Just get ready, Hales."

She gave me a beautiful smile as she went to her closet. I closed the door and went to her bed to sit down.

"Okay, I'm not sure what's going on, but I'm getting excited for it."

I smiled as she grabbed an outfit.

"You need help changing?" I asked with a devious grin.

"I think I can handle that."

"I know, but I thought you might need an extra pair of hands."

She rolled her eyes and smiled.

30 minutes later and she walked back into the room wearing a cream-colored sweater, black skinny jeans and black riding boots. She walked over to me letting me look at her outfit.

"I didn't know where we were going, so I dressed light."

"It's fine. You look good, Hales."

She went over to her desk when I stepped behind her. My hands moved down to her waist as she leaned her head back.

"I couldn't believe this was happening. I've wanted to be like this with you for a long time."

"I did too, but I thought I couldn't."

"Will you ever tell me why?" She asked while facing me. "I know because you have this loyalty towards Lamar, but..."

"There's a lot you don't know about and I would prefer to keep it that way."

"But..."

"Hayley, I really care about you, but there are some things you don't need to know."

She glanced at me as I took her hand. "We should start our night."

She nodded as she put her hand into mine and went to the door. After locking it, we went downstairs and to the exit. As soon as I pushed the double doors, Hayley squealed.

"Seriously, Morgan!"

I laughed as she ran over to my prized possession, which was my motorcycle. It was actually my dad's and it was one of the things he left me when he died. I treated it as if it was my child, because I knew how special it was to him.

"I didn't think you brought it with you here."

"I had to keep an eye on it."

Hayley laughed. "I'm sure you probably had every female but me on this bike."

I shook my head. "No; you're the only one."

She glanced at me with a surprised look. "Are you bullshiting me?"

"For such a sexy girl you have a filthy mouth."

"Look who I grew up with." She said.

"You have a point there."

"Okay, I have to get on." She said. She waited until I hopped on before taking a seat herself.

"Ready to see what tonight will bring?" I asked.

"Definitely." She replied as I cranked up the ignition. I was ready to see what was in store for tonight. Hopefully it wouldn't end up on a bad note.

***

Since we couldn't really go anywhere in the college town, I had to drive out to the city. We were pulling up into Jake's Bar when Hayley pulled away from me. Throughout the ride, I enjoyed her body pressed against mine. I wished she didn't have to pull away so soon.

"Is this one of your hangouts?" she asked while she got off the bike.

"You can say that. It's kind of my hideaway."

Hayley glanced at me as we walked inside. We went straight to the bar when a woman greeted us with a huge smile. "Wow, Morgan! I didn't expect for you to stop by."

"Hey, Aunt Doris," I said as I went behind the bar and gave her a hug. I turned to Hayley and smiled.

"Aunt Doris, this is Hayley Stevens; Hales, this is Doris, who is my mom's sister."

"Nice to meet you, Hayley. Wow, you're gorgeous. Love your hair."

Hayley blushed. "Thank you."

"Anything you want is on the house. Just let me know and I'll get it for you."

"How about a beer," Hayley suggested.

I glanced at her and shook my head.

"What, she said anything."

I handed her a soda and smiled. "That's all you're getting tonight, baby."

"I'm sure I can convince you otherwise."

"I'd like to see how."

She leaned her body onto the bar and whispered in my ear "I can do a lot in five minutes."

"As tempting as that sounds, we can do that later in your room. And trust me, it will be more than five minutes."

She bit her bottom lip as I took a bottle of beer from the cooler and took off the top.

Now, this was my type of atmosphere. The laid-back vibe was what I needed after what happened earlier. I glanced at Hayley as she moved her body to the music playing on the jukebox. I still couldn't believe Aunt Doris still had that thing. Actually, she inherited the bar from her late husband and she didn't take anything out. As for the jukebox, she added a couple of current songs onto the playlist, which was a hit for her customers.

"Let's dance."

She smiled as I put the bottle down on the bar and took her towards the dance floor. I pulled her to me as she gave me a sexy smile. Once she started dancing on me, I was gone. Everything about this girl was fucking sexy. I didn't know how I could have stayed away this long, but now that I was in her presence; I knew I wouldn't be able to leave her.

I grabbed her hips and she rolled her ass on me. Fuck, we needed to leave, now.

"You do know you're making me hard right now."

She turned around and smiled. "That was my plan to."

She suddenly stopped dancing and looked straight ahead. I looked over and saw Brandon with a group of his friends walking into the bar. I rolled my eyes and sighed. He had a smug look on his face, which only meant one thing.

"Let me go talk to him." Hayley said.

"Nah, let me."

"Morgan," Hayley said as she tried to pull me back to her.

"Stop, Hales. Nothing is going to happen. I'm going to have a friendly conversation with him."

Hayley gave me a worried look and sighed. "Okay."

I went over to the entrance with a smug look of my own. "Okay, you seen us together, so now what?"

Brandon clenched his teeth and smiled. "You do know that's my girl, right?"

"The last time I checked, she wasn't anyone's property, Brandon."

"Oh, so you can buck up to me but I bet you can't with her brother."

"You don't know what the hell I can do."

"I wouldn't talk so bold right now since I can call Lamar and tell him that you're with his sister."

I grabbed my phone out of my pocket and shoved it to him. "Go ahead and make that call."

He smiled. "I should have known about her. She ain't nothing but a fucking whore, anyway."

"I suggest you take that back." I stated as I stepped up to him.

"What the hell are you going to do?"

I punched him across his jaw and he fell backwards. Several patrons moved out of the way so they wouldn't get hit.

"Now you know what I can do!" I yelled.

He got up and tackled me, throwing me down on the floor. I got on my knees and pushed him down, holding his throat while I began punching him.

It was as if I was a different person as I continued going after him. I kept going when I felt someone's hand trying to pull me back. My hand flew back, almost hitting the person, when I realized it was Hayley.

"Morgan, stop!"

I looked at Brandon, who was nearly unconscious as one of his friends picked him up from the ground. I turned back to stare at Hayley who gave me a fearful look.

It was one of the looks I never wanted to see on her face. I never wanted her to be scared of me. Besides the pact I'd made with Lamar that was the other reason why I tried to stay away from her.

10. Hayley

After what happened with Brandon, Doris and I pulled Morgan out of the bar and into the parking lot to give him some fresh air. After a few minutes of calming down, he gave his aunt a kiss and apologized for what happened. She gave me a hug and told me to stop by anytime, which I was glad for.

Now we were heading back to my room as the wind whipped through my curls. I leaned my body against his, giving him a tight squeeze as we took in the city night. I didn't know what happened with him at Jake's. It was as if he blacked out. I didn't know if it was something that had happened to him before, but it was pretty scary to witness.

We approached my dorm in less than 30 minutes. He walked me to my room and waited for me to open the door. Once I did, he gave me a kiss on the cheek and was about to walk away when I pulled him to me.

"Where are you going?"

"I don't think I need to be with you tonight."

"I think being alone is the last thing you should do."

"Hayley..."

"Morgan, come in with me."

He sighed as I led him inside and closed the door. I took off my boots while he sat down on the bed.

"About earlier..."

"You don't have to talk about it if you don't want to."

I went over to him and sat beside him. He took my hand in his and stared at the wall.

"There's a reason why I acted the way I did."

I squeezed his hand while he looked at me. "It started after an incident when I was 16. Once it happened, I started to have periods where I would black out and I didn't remember what I did afterwards."

"Did you seek help for it?"

"I did, but it didn't work. I went to three different specialists and they couldn't find anything wrong with me. They told me it was all in my head and that I needed to confront the issue that triggered it."

"Maybe you should."

"That's not something I want to do."

"Do you want to tell me what happened?"

"I'd rather not; but there's something I wanted to do for a while now."

I glanced at him. Even though he changed the subject, I didn't mind. Hopefully he would eventually tell me what had been bothering him. "And what is that?"

"I can show you better than I can tell you."

He pulled off my sweater along with my tank. He slowly caressed my breasts, as he placed one into his mouth. I leaned my head back and sighed while he pulled on my nipple. My breath was becoming erratic as he pulled me to him. The next thing I knew, he pulled off my jeans and thong in one quick move and lay me down on the bed. He grabbed my waist and moved me towards him.

"I need to see if you taste as good as I imagined."

I smiled as I was about to lay down, but he pulled me back onto his chest.

"No, baby; with you, I want the full effect."

I became a little nervous as he pulled me down to kiss him. I may have had some sexual experience, but it was only with two guys, including Morgan. Some guys wouldn't come near me because of Lamar; so honestly, I didn't have a clue on what he wanted me to do.

He smiled as he noticed the hesitant look on my face. "Don't worry; I'm going to take good care of you."

He turned me around and leaned me forward so I was facing the wall. This position made me a little worried. What was the hell was he doing? Before I could protest, a thrilling sensation went through me as his tongue was caressing my clit. I gave a sexy moan as he rubbed my clit before going back in. I could feel him smiling underneath me as he quicken his pace. He tugged on my lips, which had me gripping the sheets.

"Shit." I whispered.

When he began flickering his tongue on me, I was gone. I began moving my hips, which had him pleasuring me even more. Before I knew it, I was screaming, letting him and everyone else know I was cumming as he gripped my waist, bringing me closer to him. I leaned my body back feeling too good to care if the guys next door heard me; that probably would be the most action they had gotten in years.

Once I was able to control myself, I lay on my side and smiled. He licked his lips while giving me a sexy smile.

"Even better than I imagined. Now, I'm addicted."

I was speechless as I lay down beside him. He kissed my lips, tasting myself, which was definitely a turn-on.

"I could tell you never done that before."

I shook my head. "I have, but not in that way."

"Hmm, so I think I need to school you on some things, if you're willing."

"With you, I wouldn't mind at all."

I leaned my body to him as he held me close. He gave a kiss to the side of my forehead and smiled against me.

No words were exchanged as we lay beside each other, enjoying the moment and finally being able to be together. This was what I had longed for; now, I would never take it for granted.

11. Morgan

A few days later, and it was time for mid-terms. Since Thanksgiving break was coming up soon, many students were anxiously counting the days down to return home. Me, not so much. I knew when I did, I would have to confront my mom, which I was dreading. I tried so hard to not think about what I'd face when I returned home, but at least Hayley would be by my side; well from a distance.

In a short time, our relationship had progressed so much, which was surreal to me. I knew she would have this effect on me. I knew I would want to spend every waking moment with her. Being near her, not wanting to let her go. And it was not just the sex that was making me crazy for her; it's just her that made me want her more and more each day. I wish I could tell someone that she was my girl, but we both agreed that maybe it wasn't the best idea to; for right now, anyway.

As for Brandon, I hadn't seen that punk since what happened at Jake's. I guess he knew not to mess with me, so he kept his distance from both Hayley and me.

Now I was at the apartment, trying to decide if I wanted to bring Hayley here later. Lamar was going out with Tamara and was possibly spending the night at her place, so we would be in the clear to spend some time here. Even though it was cool to be in her room every now and then, there were times when I rather be in my own king size bed instead of trying to sleep in her twin one. That shit was uncomfortable. Lamar walked out of his room with a duffle bag in his hand. I tried not to smile when I knew what that meant.

"Looks as if you're going out for a month instead of a night." I joked.

"I might stay at Tam's for a little bit, which would probably be cool with you."

"Why would you say that?"

"I don't know. It seems as if you've been avoiding me since you're never here anymore. Where have you been lately?"

I shrugged and went into the kitchen. "Just around."

"You met someone, haven't you? It must be serious if you're spending all your time with her."

"You can say that."

"Who is she?"

I gave a slight smile as I went into the refrigerator. I slowly looked inside, hoping he would get off of this subject.

"You can tell me; we're boys, remember."

"We are, but this is something I want to keep to myself for a while. I don't want to jinx it."

Lamar gave me a weird look and sighed. "I guess you're right. I mean, you haven't been like this with a girl since, well hell, never. You always fucked them and leave."

"Well, I guess you rubbed off on me some."

"I guess so. It's good that you have finally changed; going from girl to girl gets old real quick."

"Yeah, it does."

"So, you are going back home for Thanksgiving, are you?" Lamar asked.

"Yeah; why wouldn't I?"

"I dunno. The days you have been here, you have been out of it. I know you are a little hesitant about going."

I glanced at him and sighed. A flashback of me pointing a gun came to mind as I stared at the window. I shook my head as I went to sit down on the barstool.

"Are you okay, man?"

"Yeah, I'm cool."

"Oh, and Braxton came by and dropped off your chem book. I put it in your room."

"Thanks."

"You sure you're okay, Mo?"

I saw a younger version of myself still holding the gun. I don't know why I was thinking about that, but hopefully it'll stop soon.

"I'm fine. You get out of here and spend time with Tam."

"Alright. Later."

I nodded as he walked out of the door. I leaned back on the barstool, trying to figure out why I would be thinking about that. That was something I'd been trying to push in the back of my mind for years. It had worked for a while, but after what happened at Jake's I had been thinking about it more.

I shook my head again and went into my room. I couldn't think about this, especially when Hayley came over. I wanted to focus all of my time on her, so my thoughts would have to take a back seat for now. If I could.

***

After I knew for sure Lamar has left, I called Hayley to let her know I was swinging by to pick her up, but she insisted on driving her car there. I really didn't want her to do that, especially if Lamar decided to come back, but since she was already out, she figured she would come straight there.

A couple of minutes later and she arrived. As soon as I opened the door, I grabbed her waist, pulling her into the apartment. She wrapped her legs around me as I leaned her against the wall.

"I see you're anxious to see me." Hayley said while smiling.

"I'm always anxious to see you, baby."

She kissed me as I took her over to the couch. I still had her wrapped around me as she straddled me and quickly pulled off my shirt.

"Did you at least want to eat first?" I asked.

"We can do that later." She said and unbuttoned my jeans. I hiked her dress to her waist as she glanced at me.

"Condom?"

"Of course." I said. I went into my pocket and took one out. She took it from me, tore off the wrapper and inserted it on me.

My hands slowly touched her shoulders as she leaned into me. We stared at each other, taking in the moment between each other. Since the time we have spent together, I realized I was falling hard for her. Shit, I think I was in love with her even before we got together; but now, those feelings were there and I couldn't deny them anymore.

She started moving her hips as she slowly took off her dress. She was completely naked as I smiled.

"You walked out of your room with nothing on underneath?"

"That's because I was coming to you."

"I don't know if I should be upset or turned on even more?"

"You could always go for the second option." She said and leaned into me. Her hands gripped the couch as my hands went to her ass. She gave a blissful sigh as my fingers lightly touched her back. I leaned her back while I sucked on her breasts as her hips continued to rock against me.

Without even disconnecting, I pulled her up and lay her down on the couch. I admired her body as she looked into my eyes. I didn't know if this was the right moment to say it, but I was going to.

"I love you, Hales."

She glanced at me not knowing what to say as I dived in. She was exactly how I wanted her to be nice, wet, and tight. Everything about this girl was perfect, which for me, could be a bad thing, especially if we ever broke up. I would probably lose my damn mind if that ever happened.

She continued to stare at me as she grabbed the back of my neck.

"I love you too, Morgan."

I pulled her back up without even breaking our stride. Her tits jiggled as she held onto me. She was riding my dick so good I had to control myself. I wanted her to get hers in first before I did.

She leaned back, grabbing her breasts, letting me know she was cumming. That was a beautiful sight to see.

She leaned towards me and kissed me before going back at it again. She touched my chest as she bent down and kissed my neck. She was matching me with every move, which meant she was definitely a keeper.

I was reaching my climax as she was reaching hers for the second time. She held onto me as her body shook against mine. She stared at me and smiled.

"I really do love you." I said.

"Why, because I can get you off good?"

I laughed. "Well, you definitely have that going for you, but it's not that. You're just perfect. That's why I would never in my life hurt you. You deserve so much and I hope I can be the man to give you everything and more."

Hayley looked away from me, trying to hide her tears from me. I tilted her head back to me and wiped her tears from her cheeks.

We continued to stare at each other when the door suddenly opened. We both couldn't move as the door closed and the sound of heels were clicking on the hardwood floor.

Once we were finally able to regain any feeling in our legs, Hayley jumped up to grab her dress while I put my shirt back on.

"Oh my God!" Tamara yelled as she turned around to face the door.

"It's not what it looks like." Hayley said.

"I didn't see anything. In fact, you didn't even see me here."

"Why are you here anyway?" I asked while zipping up my jeans.

"Lamar forgot his economics book; since I was in the area, I told him I would come by and get it."

"I forgot you had a key. Fuck!" I exclaimed.

"Listen, if you two think I'll tell Lamar about this, I won't. In fact, I'm kind of glad you two are together."

We both glanced at her while she smiled. "Just because I'm with Lamar does not mean I agree with his way of thinking. I've tried countless times to convince him to loosen the brother grip on you, Hales; but he won't even listen to me."

"Wow, thanks Tam."

She smiled. "No problem; but there is something I need to ask."

We both looked at her while she gave an unsure look.

"Honestly, I don't even know if I should ask this."

"What is it?" Hayley asked.

"Did something happen in your past that is making Lamar act this way? He's so possessive with you as if he's trying to shield you from something."

I glanced at Hayley, who gave Tamara a slight shrug.

"No. Lamar has always been this way; it's just how he is."

She shook her head. "Well, maybe I could do some more convincing, because he needs to let you two live your life and I'm pretty sure sneaking around will get old eventually."

She went over to the entertainment center and picked up Lamar's book. She looked at Hayley and gave her a hug.

She looked at me and smiled. "Treat her right, okay."

"You know I will."

She glanced at us again before going to the door.

We both looked at each other as Hayley went to the couch to sit down.

"Wow. What if that was Lamar that came in here? He probably would have killed us both."

"Hales, maybe it's time that we told him. Yeah, he'll be pissed and probably will want to kill me, but at least everything would be out in the open."

"I know, but I just have this feeling that things will get out of control. Although my brother can be a pain in the ass majority of the time, I don't want your friendship to be ruined. You're like a brother to him and this will devastate him."

"I know; trust me, I have a lot to think about if we are exposed, but Tamara's right. We're going to get tired of sneaking around. Hell, I'm feeling like that right now. I'm ready to face whatever happens between Lamar and me."

Hayley glanced at me. "Really?"

"Yeah. I said I'll fight for you to the end; I'm not going back on my word."

Hayley came over to me and wrapped her arms around me.

I sighed as I touched her hair. I knew what I just told her was somewhat true, but I had a lot at stake if Lamar found out about us. Now, I was willing to take that risk just to be with her.

12. Lamar

I parked my car in the parking spot in front of Tamara's apartment and sighed. Since she wanted me to spend a couple of days with her, I was fine by it, but I really needed to be alone and think. When I was talking to Morgan earlier, I sensed something was up with him. He hadn't been himself, so it kind of had me curious. I knew it had something to do with this new girl he's seeing, which I still didn't know who she was, but whomever it was, it was always making him jumpy.

I looked over and Tamara's car pulling up. She glanced over at me and smiled as she turned off the ignition. I grabbed my bag and got out of the car.

"Hey." I said as I kissed her.

"Hope you weren't waiting long."

"No, not really. It didn't matter anyway since I needed some time to think."

"About what?"

"Some things I've noticed lately with Mo."

Tamara gave a hesitant look as she pulled out my economics book.

"Thanks for getting that for me. Was Morgan there when you went by?"

"He actually was. With his girl. I kind of interrupted them while they were..."

"Whoa. I'm sure that was awkward."

"Very." Tamara whispered as she walked in front of me to the apartment.

I gave Tamara a weird look as she opened the door. "Is there something I should know?"

She turned around and smiled. "Why would you think that?"

"Because that look you have right now. You only do that when you're hiding something."

"Mar, you know if something was up, I would tell you, right?"

"You would, but if it's something that you're trying to hide, you wouldn't tell me."

"I'm not hiding anything. Remember, we tell each other everything."

I nodded and sighed. "Sorry, Tam, I guess I'm just being paranoid."

"Why?"

I went over to the couch and sat down. "I think something is up with Morgan. He hasn't been himself lately and for some reason, I think it has to do with Hales."

"You don't say." She said.

"Is there something you know about the two?"

"Like I said before, I'm not hiding anything. Speaking of Hayley, don't you think you need to leave her alone? I mean, she's a grown woman."

"So what if she is; she's still my sister."

"She's two years younger than you, Mar, so I categorize that as being grown. You need to let her live her life."

"Did she tell you something?"

"She didn't tell me anything. It's just what I see when I'm around you two. How can she be able to live when you're constantly underneath her telling her what to do?"

"Because she needs to be protected."

"From what? Have you ever wondered if she was in any sort of danger or needed to confide in you that she probably won't because of the way you're treating her now?"

I sighed. "I never thought about it like that."

"Well, maybe you should."

"If you understood where I'm coming from, then you would feel the same way."

Tamara stared at me. "Did something happen that made you be this way towards Hales?"

I sighed. A lot of things had happened that made me do the things I did regarding Hayley. I didn't know if I should even tell Tamara about it, since she probably wouldn't understand.

"Is everything okay?" Tamara asked as she gave me a concerned look.

"Yeah, everything's cool. One more thing about Hales?"

"What?"

"Has she been spending time with Morgan? I know he helped her out at Onyx."

"I guess they have been. Why would you ask that?"

"Just wondering. Actually, I need to head back to the apartment for a bit. There's something else I forgot."

Tamara's eyes grew wide as she stared at me. "What did you forget? I could go get it."

"Why? I can get it. It's no big deal. Besides, I was going to head to the store and get some things for later."

"What's for later?"

I smiled and gave her a kiss. "You'll see."

She gave a hesitant look and I went to the door. I'm not sure why she didn't want me to leave, but I couldn't worry about that. For some reasons, my imagination was running wild. I didn't know why, but I have a feeling that maybe things were not what they seemed with Hayley and Morgan. And now, I think I needed to confirm onto whether what I'm thinking was actually true.

***

Fifteen minutes later and I was back at my place. I opened the door, wondering if Morgan was here, but he probably was out since I didn't see his bike out front. I slowly walked inside. I didn't know why I was paranoid. I knew I shouldn't have thought that way about him and Hayley. I mean, he made a promise to me that he wouldn't even look at her, let alone talk to her, so what I was thinking could be way off base. He knew better, especially after what I'd done for him.

I went over to the entertainment center when I suddenly stopped. I looked over at the couch and saw something shiny on the cushion. I went closer, noticing it was Hayley's bracelet that she had since she was 15. I picked it up, wondering why it was here. I hadn't seen Hayley since the confrontation in her room, so she never came to the apartment, unless...

"Nah, he promised." I said.

I went into his room, seeing if there was anything else that I could find that was Hayley's. I went through his things, but I couldn't find anything. Anger was rising in me at the idea of Hayley and Morgan being together. I did something for him that I used to help me with my crusade for Morgan to think twice about touching her, so if he ever went back on his word, I would definitely exposed his ass.

If those two were together, not only were they doing it behind my back, but the idea that they were doing it here was really pissing me off. I couldn't stand liars, which is why I was going to have to address it to the both of them.

Honestly, I don't like how I was treating Hales. I mean, she probably thought that I was crazy, but it was for her own good. She has such a bright future and I didn't want anything to interfere with that. Too many issues had occurred to the people that were important to me and I didn't want her to be another victim. If I have to be a crazed ass brother to her, then so be it. At least I knew she would be safe and alive.

An idea popped into my head as I went into my room. I searched through my things until I found my camcorder. I haven't used that thing in years, only because it made me think about an incident that happened years ago. Honestly, I hadn't touched once since that incident occurred, but I thought for a small second, I could slowly let it go.

I went back into Morgan's room and looked for a convenient, but hard to see area that would show Morgan and possibly Hayley admitting they were together. The one thing I didn't want to see were the two of them fucking. I think I would lose my mind if they were.

Don't get me wrong, I love Morgan like a brother. The two of us have been great friends and have confided in each other over everything. He had helped me with my parents' divorce, while I helped him through the issues with his stepfather. That's why it would hurt me if those two were hooking up behind my back, because that showed he wasn't being honest with me.

I went over to his night stand drawer, quickly put in the camcorder and left the drawer open a bit. He didn't usually go into them for anything, so that should have been an okay spot to put it. The only thing was having the recorder on at all times, but how else would I be able to expose the two without constantly having it on?

I sighed, looking around his room one last time before I left. I needed to get out before he suddenly returned.

I closed the door and looked ahead, knowing what I was doing was wrong, but those two didn't leave me any choice. I had to know the truth and if I had to invade my boy's privacy, then whatever.

13. Hayley

A week after Tamara discovered Morgan and me together; I was now getting ready for Thanksgiving week. I received my last mid-term grade, which was for physics, with an 80. Not bad. Hopefully I could keep this up because finals were just around the corner and I did not need to be delayed from graduating.

I was waiting on Paula to arrive so we could head on the road when my phone beeped. I picked it up from the bed and saw that it was a text from Morgan. The words "I love you" were etched across the screen, which made me smile. Who knew he could be sentimental? I'm not sure if he ever said those words to another female, besides his mom of course, but it did make me feel pretty special. Honestly, I think I was in love with him even before we became a couple. Now, I didn't have to wonder anymore about us being together; I knew it would be exactly how I imagined it.

I stared at my reflection in the mirror and noticed the glow I had on my skin. Damn, I didn't know being in love would do that to you. Although this new experience was a little scary, it was also exciting to see what else was in store for us.

There was a knock at the door. I figured since it was Paula, I told her to come in. Sure enough, it was her, coming in with two big suitcases.

"What's with the suitcases? We're only going back for a week."

"I know, but I need different outfits if I get bored and need something different."

"Don't you have clothes at home?"

"I brought everything here."

I shook my head and went back to looking in the mirror.

She came over to me and smiled. "Look at you. Morgan must be putting it on you good for you to be glowing like that."

I turned around and blushed. "Am I that obvious?"

"Very. At least he finally wised up and saw you for the wonderful woman that you are. So I guess Lamar really doesn't have his balls, huh?"

I laughed. "Not at all,"

"I'm really happy for you, Hales. You have been in love with him since you first laid eyes on him, so it's great that your dream came true."

"It is, isn't it?"

Paula gave a slight nod and sat down on the bed.

"Hey, is everything okay?"

She gave me a bright smile. "Everything's cool, sort of. Scott broke up with me."

"What?! Why?"

"I guess he felt I was too much for him. I don't know why he thought that. So what if I wanted to spend all of my time with him, that's what people in relationships do, right?"

"That's true."

"I guess he thought I was being clingy. Can you picture me being clingy?"

"Not really." I replied.

"Exactly my point. Anyway, at least you have Morgan now, who I have to admit looks mighty fine since you two been together."

"Morgan was always fine."

"If you say so." She laughed.

I glanced at her, realizing what she had just said. I quickly blocked that out of my mind as I grabbed my jacket from the desk chair.

"We better head out if we don't want to be in traffic."

Paula agreed and grabbed her suitcases. I picked up my duffle bag and sighed. I knew once we were off campus, Morgan and I would have an even harder time seeing each other. But we would find some way to make it work.

***

Once we got through the campus traffic, we were out on the road heading to Houston. I sighed, not sure if I wanted to go home. I didn't know if I wanted to be under the same roof with Lamar. Sure, we went to the same college, but we didn't see each other often, unless he wanted to bother me. Now, I had to look at him for the entire week, which was making me kind of pissed.

After the two hour drive, we were in the city. Once I approached Paula's house, I told her we could hang out later, which was fine by her. 20 minutes later and I was at mine, standing in the driveway, trying to collect my thoughts before going inside.

I had to prepare myself for what was ahead. I'm sure soon as I walked in, I would see my mom and possibly my dad, sitting on the couch probably making out or doing a lot more. Even though they were divorced, there were time when they slipped back into relationship mode, or what I thought was the banging mode. One minute they couldn't stand each other and the next they were all over each other. They were a complicated bunch, but they were my parents.

I went to the door and opened it with my key. To my surprise, my mom was in the kitchen, alone, making dinner.

"Hey, sweetie." She said as she came over to me for a hug.

"Hey, Mom. So I see you're cooking?"

"Yes; actually, I'm making chicken enchiladas for both you and Lamar. I also told him to invite Morgan to dinner."

My heart skipped a beat when she mentioned Morgan. I didn't know how I was going to act with him being in the same room with Lamar and my parents. Hopefully he didn't accept the invite, but knowing him, he would.

"Great. Did you need any help?"

"No. All I want you to do is put your feet up and relax."

"Thanks, but I rather be doing something constructive."

She sighed and came over to me. "Spill."

I glanced at her. "What are you talking about?"

"Please, I gave birth to you, so I know when you're hiding something."

"It's nothing, Mom."

"Is it a certain person by the name of Morgan the reason you're all jumpy? I saw that look on your face when I mentioned his name."

I sighed. Nothing got passed her.

"Yeah. We're seeing each other."

My mom gave me a surprised look as she sat down. "Seriously?"

"Yeah. It's been a couple of weeks now, but we're a couple."

"Wow. I really didn't think that would happen, especially since Lamar is so hell bent on you not being with anyone."

"Which I still need to know why. Even you and Dad can't get him to stop."

"He doesn't know, does he?"

I shook my head and sighed.

"Hales..."

"Before you said anything, Mom, you know our positions. You know he would go through the roof if he knew."

"He will, but it's best if he knows now about it before someone tells him."

"And who would tell him?"

"It could be someone you least expect, sweetie. I just don't want you getting into a situation that you can't get out of. Lamar and Morgan have been friends since they were five and you getting into a relationship with him will break that friendship up."

"But why should it be like that? Lamar should be happy that I'm dating his friend."

"Lamar doesn't look at it that way. Instead, he's seeing all the things Morgan has done in his past, including dating multiple girls. He doesn't want you to get hurt."

"I understand that, but he's taking the big brother routine too far. Besides, Morgan wouldn't hurt me. In fact, he told me he loves me."

My mom gave a sweet smile as she put an arm around me. "Now that, I can see. He always has had a soft spot for you, and now, he's finally letting everything go to be with you."

"I know. I just wish Lamar could be more open to us being together."

My mom gave me a pat on the back and went to the counter.

"Does this means Dad is coming too?"

"Maybe."

"What is really going on with you two? Your relationship is so weird."

My mom smiled. "I guess only time will tell, sweetie."

I sighed as my phone beeped. I pulled it out of my pocket and saw it was a text from Morgan. It read for me to wear a dress tonight. I don't know why that was so important, but I guess for him I would.

"It may not seem like it will, but everything will work out Hales."

I nodded and my mom continued cooking. I knew she meant well, but nothing good would come out of Morgan and me telling Lamar about us. Although, I told Morgan to admit his feelings to me, I think he needed to keep quiet about everything, because I knew when that day did come; someone was going to end up hurt or possibly dead.

***

After helping my mom with dinner, I went to my room and took a shower. I missed having my own bathroom. The community showers were horrible, so I could enjoy this week of luxury.

I put on a blue and white striped sweater dress and matched it with a pair of black riding boots. I stared at myself in the mirror, satisfied with my look, as I went downstairs to wait on the guys to arrive.

10 minutes later and the door opened. Lamar and Morgan walked in and I swear I let out a moan.

Damn, he is fine. His eyes stared intensely at me as a sexy smile slowly went across his lips.

My phone beeped as I was receiving a text. I reached into my pocket and read it, squeezing my thighs together as he wrote how much he wanted his favorite meal. Of course he wasn't talking about food. I replied back, letting him know he could have it anytime he wanted. He looked at his phone, rubbed his chin and replied back. I glanced at his message, saying definitely later, which I nodded.

Hopefully we weren't being too obvious around each other, because Lamar was definitely giving us looks. If we wanted this to continue, we had to be discreet, so I quickly walked into the dining room to help my mom set the table.

A few seconds later and my dad walked in. He gave me a hug and kissed my cheek.

"Hi baby girl."

"Hey, Dad. How are things going?"

"Great. Business is booming as usual."

"That's great to hear."

"You do know when you graduate next year, there is a position for you at the company."

I glanced at my dad and sighed. There was no way I was working in the family business. My dad owned a computer tech company which was very lucrative, since he worked for various businesses in the city. Lamar had already landed a position there, so I did not want to work alongside him. Besides, I had another career option in mine, which was also my major: entertainment management.

When my parents first found out my major, they weren't too pleased, but event planning is something I wanted to do. And what would be better than planning events for celebrities? It was going to happen, and it was something I was striving for.

"Dad, I already told you I do not want a position with the company. I have no desire to have any stake in the corporation."

"Why not? Lamar did. Besides, you don't have to be a technician; you could work within the business by being an executive."

"Thanks, but no thanks."

"Leave her alone, Cedric. She has already made it clear she doesn't want to be in the business."

My dad sighed and I smiled. He went over to my mom and kissed her neck.

"I have to ask, are you two getting back together?"

They both looked at me with unsure glances. "We like how things are between us." My dad said and went over to the wine rack. I guess that answered my question.

While my dad acknowledged Lamar and Morgan, I went to take a seat at the table. Morgan sat down beside me while Lamar sat on the opposite end. I would have thought Lamar would have a problem with that, but I guess not.

"Will Tamara be joining us?" My mom asked.

"No. Her parents wanted to spend time with her, so they're taking her out for dinner."

"So Morgan, how's everything going with your classes?" My dad asked.

"It's going great, Mr. Stevens. I passed all of my mid-terms, so I'm just waiting on the semester to end."

"I'm sure. Have a new girlfriend these days."

He smiled and nodded. "Yeah, I do. She's an amazing woman and I can see myself being with her for a long time."

I hope my cheeks were not burning red right now. I glanced over at my mom, who gave a tiny smile while taking a sip of wine.

"I definitely have to meet this girl, if you're saying all of that." Lamar said while grabbing his glass of lemonade.

I cleared my throat and also took a sip of mine. That wasn't happening anytime soon.

Morgan dropped his napkin on the floor. He bent down and picked it up. Before I knew it, his hand was on my thigh, giving it a slight caress to calm me down. He continued to move his hand further, which had me surprised. I wanted to look at him, but I didn't want to give myself away, so I stared ahead. I bit my lip as his touch hit my clit. While he was acting calm, I was terrified, yet a bit turned on by what he was doing. I didn't want to start moaning, so I took another sip of my drink, so I could distract myself from what was happening.

He spread my legs and one of his fingers went deep in me. My eyes closed as I was trying hard not to react. I gripped the bottom of the tablecloth as I was about to cum. I couldn't believe this was happening, but it felt so damn good.

My hand was in a tight fist as a wave went through me. My body shook as I leaned back in my chair shivering from what I just experienced.

Morgan pulled out his napkin from underneath him and pretended like nothing even happened.

"Are you okay, baby girl?" My dad asked.

"Yeah, I don't know why I'm cold of all a sudden."

Morgan glanced at me and hid the smile that was forming.

"Here," he said as he draped his jacket over my shoulders. I smiled and pulled it close to me. Lamar stared at us with a curious glance.

Morgan excused himself from the table to go to the bathroom. I wanted so bad to follow him, but I didn't want to be obvious. That and I couldn't move anyway since my legs were still weak from what happened.

"You sure everything is okay? Your face is kind of flushed." My mom asked.

"I'm fine, couldn't be better." I said.

I needed for dinner to be over so I could be with Morgan and return the favor for him.

14. Morgan

After what I did to Hayley at the table, I had to be with her. I knew I shouldn't have done that, but she was looking too good in that dress. And I could tell she was a little nervous, so I was doing my best to calm her down. Instead, it had me fucking horny.

After dinner, I texted her, asking her to meet me at my house. I had somewhere I wanted to take her so we could be alone. She replied, saying she would leave in 30 minutes.

I told everyone I was leaving, which Lamar was disappointed. I guess he wanted to hang out. Not tonight.

I arrived to my house and walked into the living room to see my mom sitting in her favorite armchair. That was the only chair she would sit in.

I went over to her and gave her a kiss on the cheek. She didn't even acknowledge me as she stared at the wall.

I scratched the back of my head and sighed. I didn't know if I should talk to her or just go in my room. There were days when she was like that and days when she was not. It all happened after the incident when I was 16. I tried to help her in any way that I could, but there were some times when even I couldn't do it. That's why I went off to college; not only to receive an education, but to get away from the issues I had at home.

Honestly, I didn't even know if she knew I was at home as I looked around the room.

"Mom,"

She finally looked over and saw me. "Hi Morgan. When did you get here?"

I smiled. "I just did."

She gave me a worried glance. "I tried calling you recently."

"I know and I'm sorry. I was just busy with school."

I felt guilty lying to her. Even though I had issues myself with what happened, I should had answered the phone and talked to her.

"Well, you're here now." She said and smiled.

"How are you feeling?"

"Good."

I didn't want to say too much, so I just nodded.

"I did want to talk about that night, Morgan."

I glanced at the TV. I knew this was going to happen, that's why I didn't want to come home.

"Mom, please."

"Morgan, I know it took a lot from you and even for me too. I haven't been the same since, but just know that I would never blame you for what happened. It was something you had to do."

"I really don't want to talk about this."

"Morgan…"

"I said I don't want to talk about it!" I exclaimed.

My mom looked scared as she leaned back in her chair. I closed my eyes, knowing I shouldn't have done that.

"I'm really sorry. I didn't mean to yell, Mom."

She slowly got up and went to her room and closed the door. I sighed, knowing what that meant. She would probably be in there for days. I would have to bring her food so she could eat and tell her when to sleep. I didn't know how much more I could take of this. I loved my mom, but we both needed to get pass what happened.

I went outside and went to my car. I texted Hayley to let her know to meet me at the restaurant near my house. I couldn't have her coming here just in case anything else occurred.

***

After arriving at the diner, I waited in the parking lot for Hayley. A few minutes later, her Toyota Corolla pulled up beside my car. She got out and came over to me.

"Hey, why did you want to meet here?"

"I didn't want to disturb my mom."

"Okay, I'll follow you."

I nodded and she got back into her car.

After 20 minutes, we arrived at our destination. I got out of the car as I waited for her to pull up behind me. She got out of hers and slowly looked around.

"Where are we?"

"I'll tell you in a second. Come on." I replied.

She walked in front of me as we went to the door. She looked around again before I opened the door. I turned on the light switch and Hayley gasped.

"Wow, this place is beautiful."

She walked in even further and took in the cream and beige walls, the tan furniture and the beautiful view of the lake overlooking the area.

"It was my stepfather's."

She turned around and stared at me. "Really?"

"Yeah. Remember, he was a developer, so he had a lot of property. This was one of them."

"Why would you bring me here? I know you and him really didn't get along."

I sighed. That was true that we didn't, but that didn't mean I wouldn't use his place. This was kind of my getaway spot when I was younger. Whenever I had an issue with my mom, this would be where I came to think. The only other person who knew about this place was Lamar, and that was because he wanted to find a place for him and Tamara to be alone.

My stepfather and I had a difficult relationship. We had never seen eye to eye on various things. He tried to be my father when he wasn't. He could have never been him and I made that known every single day.

"He designed the place, but he never stayed here. The model was completed before he died, though. He never really paid attention to it since he had others."

"What made this one so special for you to go to?"

"Because he never set foot in it."

"And why no one ever bought the place?"

"Why so many questions?"

"Just curious."

"No one ever bought this place or any of his properties because they went to my mom. She never had the heart to get rid of them, so she kept this one and two others."

"Oh."

"Now, can we stop talking about him and focus on us?"

Hayley smiled and put her arms around me.

"You know you were looking too damn sexy at dinner, especially when I was making you cum."

"Which you shouldn't have done. I couldn't believe you."

"I couldn't resist. Besides, no one noticed what I was doing."

She began to play with my hair as I grabbed her ass. She leaned over and kissed my neck.

"What else did you want to do?"

"Let's see. I would have moved all the food off of the table, lay you down, spread your legs, and had my meal."

"What's stopping you now?"

"Not a damn thing." I said as I pulled her up. She wrapped her legs around me as I took her into the bedroom. Hopefully she hadn't told everyone she wasn't coming back tonight, because she was going to be with me for the entire night.

***

"What are you thinking about?"

I looked over at Hayley who was staring at me. She looked beautiful at the moment. She pushed a curl from her face and laid her cheek on her hand. Her leg was slowly touching mine, as I touched her shoulder. After getting what I wanted, she did the same for me, which I enjoyed. I didn't know she had that in her, but I guess I'm sort of rubbing off some of freakiness on her. Now I had to bring down the mood by doing something I didn't want to do, and that was think about my past.

"It's not anything."

"You know you can talk to me, right?

I touched her hair and she smiled. "I was thinking about what happened when I was younger. Before my mom met Craig, we had a good life. It would have been perfect if my dad was alive, but we kept everything together. When he came along, everything started to go downhill. My mom wasn't the vibrant, wonderful woman she was; instead, she became a shadow of herself, catering to his every want and need. He tried to make me into his servant, which even at 10, that shit wasn't happening. We used to get into arguments, which sometimes turned physical. That was why I was always at your house. Even though it wasn't hard to not come around your family, I was mainly escaping all the shit that was happening."

Hayley glanced at me and touched my cheek. I held her hand and lightly kissed her fingers.

"Was he abusive towards your mom?"

I lowered my head and took a deep breath. "Yeah. There were times when I heard them argue and the next day she would appear with a bruise or a black eye. When I tried to come to her defense, she would shield me, telling me not to fight her battles. I mean, why would she want me to stand around and watch her husband beat her? She was my mom and I wanted to protect her."

"Which you should had. I think she wanted you to not be involved because she felt she should been protecting you instead."

I sighed and lay down. "I'm just glad he's gone. Even though the damage has been done, at least he won't be able to hurt us anymore."

Hayley gave me a concerned look while I stared at the wall. Another memory of me holding the gun came to mind.

I did what I had to do to protect myself and my mom. Although it caused a lot of grief, I would do it again if I had to.

15. Lamar

Since Morgan didn't want to hang out after dinner, I spent some time with my parents; even though that wasn't a bad thing. My parents weren't the typical parents. For starters, their relationship status was up in the air. One minute, those two were together and the next they weren't. I think it has something to do with the fact they both wanted to date other people while still able to sleep with each other. That was just weird and awkward.

While my dad was on a phone call, my mom sat down beside me and smiled.

"Is everything okay with you? You were kind of quiet at dinner."

"Everything's cool, Mom. Just have a lot to think about."

"You know you can talk to me, right?"

"I know, but this I rather keep to myself."

"This doesn't have anything to do with Hayley, does it?"

I looked ahead as she sighed. "Lamar, how many times do I have to tell you that you need to let this obsession with protecting her go? She's a grown woman and she can pretty much handle her own. I mean, she can fight men bigger than you and probably better than you."

I laughed. "Maybe so."

"I know you still think about Samantha, Lamar. What happened to her was tragic, but you can't let that get you down nor let it ruin your relationship with Hayley. What happened to Samantha will not happen to Hales."

"You don't know that, Mom. I was supposed to have seen Samantha that night. I should have been with her, but she was so stubborn and went on her own. That's how Hayley is and I don't want anything bad to happen with her."

"There's so much hurt and pain in you that you don't even realize it."

I sighed, wondering when my mom would stop talking about this. I really didn't want to think about that day at all.

"You and Morgan are so much alike. I know something happened to him that completely changed him, just like the incident with Samantha for you."

"Yeah, I know."

"So don't you think you need to let things go and to let Morgan live his life."

I glanced at my mom. "What do you mean by that? Why do you think Morgan's not living his life?"

My mom sighed. "All I'm saying is you need to try and focus on your life and not worry about everyone else's. I know that night took a toll on you mentally and it's causing problems with you, Hayley, and even Morgan."

"I don't know what Morgan has to do with this."

My mom put an arm around me and sighed. "Just try and let some things go; it will do you a world of good if you did."

I gave my mom a doubtful look as she patted my back and got up. I shook my head, wondering if she was trying to hint at something. If she was talking about Morgan and Hayley, then I had that under control. Hopefully, I was already getting certain signs that there was something going on, but I needed confirmation before I put a foot in Morgan's ass.

And if he was banging my sister, I wouldn't think twice about beating him down.

16. Morgan

March, 2008

I sat inside my car in front of the house, wondering if I should go inside. Coming to this house was starting to be an issue every single day. I will be so glad when I turn 18 so I can get the fuck out of this environment and be on my own. I can't continue staying here and being in this constant shit with Craig. He's an idiot and I'd rather not be around him. But my mom loves him, so I don't have a choice.

My mom met Craig a year after my dad passed away from cancer. I missed him so much. He was definitely my rock. He was a great person and had a heart of gold; something that Craig definitely didn't have. Really, I don't know what in the hell my mom sees in Craig. I don't know if she was lonely and needed someone in her life or what, but she could have done so much better than that loser.

When they first met, they were strictly friends. They talked about their problems and he made her happy. Five years later, when I was 10, he proposed to her, which was the worst day of my life. I couldn't believe he was trying to be a part of our lives permanently and it killed me when she accepted his proposal.

Craig was what I would call a smooth-talker, but actually he was a punk ass. He danced his way into my mom's life, treated her good at first, but once they really got involved, that was when he had changed into this crazy ass lunatic that wanted everything done his way. I knew what he was about from day one so that's probably why he didn't like me. Well, the feelings were mutual.

I continued to stare at the garage, wondering if I should just start up the car and go somewhere when a text came through my phone. I glanced at it and saw that it was Lamar, wondering what I was doing. I texted him back, letting him know I was about to head inside the house when he replied, saying if I needed to hang out at his then I could. I smiled, knowing my friend meant well. He knew how my home situation was, so he tried everything he could to help me get through it. I was blessed that I was able to have someone like him in my life. He has been more than a friend to me; he was family.

My smile grew wider when I thought about Lamar's sister, Hayley. I could go by there to see her. Damn, I wanted one second to kiss her. I bet she's a good kisser, among other things. Shit, now I'm hard. I quickly readjusted myself, hoping I don't have a boner when I went inside, but she has that type of effect on me.

I sighed and got out of the car. I might as well get this over with. I went to the door and used my key to open it. I walked inside and saw the living room in a sea of candles. My mom was near the table standing as she smoothed down her dress. She turned around to stare at me.

"Oh, hi sweetie I thought you were Craig."

I rolled my eyes as I threw my keys on the counter. "Sorry to disappoint you. Why are you planning something for him? Shouldn't he be doing that for you since it's your birthday?"

"It doesn't matter who plans what. I just wanted to do something special, so I decided to do it today."

I sighed. Probably because he wouldn't have done anything anyway.

"Could you help me move this table, please?"

I sighed. I really didn't want to, but for my mom, I'll do anything for her.

After moving the table, bringing out the food, and helping her with a couple of other items, the living room was transformed into a romantic setting which in my opinion that bastard didn't deserve. My mom was doing too much for him and I hated it.

I glanced around and grabbed my keys. "Anything else?"

"No. Thank you, sweetie for helping me. I know you didn't want to do it."

"You know I would have for you, Mom. He doesn't deserve you."

"Morgan, stop. He's my husband."

"Well, he's doing a pissed poor job of it. He's barely here, doing who knows what and when he is, he's controlling you and trying to do the same with me, which will never happen."

"That's enough, Morgan. He's never home because he's at work the majority of the time. When he is here, he just wants to unwind and not have to do anything; that is when my duty as a wife comes in to help him distress from his day."

I glanced at my mom, wondering what happened to the strong, independent woman that I remembered. Instead, she's a shadow of herself. She was going through the motions to satisfy that jackass.

"I understand that you were lonely when Dad passed, but you should have really thought twice before getting involved with Craig. He's a manipulator and he will continue to be one because you're allowing him to be."

"You don't know what you're talking about, Morgan."

"Maybe not; I'm just basing it on what I see every day."

The door opened and I rolled my eyes. I was trying to leave before he came home.

I turned around and stared at the man who had made my life a living hell. He gave me a cold stare as he walked into the room.

"Why the hell are there so many candles? Did we pay the light bill?"

"I just thought we could have a romantic evening together. You know today is my birthday, right?" My mom asked. Her eyes gave a pleading look, hoping that he remembered.

He scoffed as he sat down on the couch. "Oh, I did forget. Sorry."

She gave a sad look as she went to the table. I shook my head. I was really getting tired of this shit.

"Since you're up, could you bring me a beer? And maybe fix some dinner. I'm starving."

"Sure. I made..."

"I don't want what you made. I'm in the mood for a big steak and potatoes, so if you can fix that, then you will receive a big smile from me as a birthday present."

I smirked at his stupid remark. I wished I could shove my foot up his ass. Punk.

"I'll get that for you, then."

That was it! I went over to him and gave him a heated look.

"You need to apologize to my mom."

He looked at me and smirked. "For what?"

"For being a fucking prick! My mom has been nothing but good to you and she just asked for one day, but of course, you have to make it all about you."

"I don't know who you think you're talking to, but you better go sit your ass down."

"Or what? What the hell are you going to do to me? Trust me, whatever you would do, you wouldn't get far."

"You don't know what I'm capable of."

"Stop it, you two! Morgan, stop defying Craig. I'll start on your steak, sweetie. I think we have one left in the freezer."

"Mom, you do not have to do that. You cooked a wonderful dinner. If he's hungry enough, he'll eat that."

"Who asked for your opinion? I'm the one making the money around here, so whatever I want, I should get it!"

"You may make the money, but my mom is the one who has kept this household going. In fact, this is not even your damn house! It's from what my dad left us when he died. You just decided to move your ass into our place."

"Well, who kept it afloat?"

"You know what, I don't need to hear this anymore. You will always be a prick." I said as I went to the door.

"Honestly Morgan, do you even know who your dad is? I mean, for all we know, he might not even be dead."

I turned around and stared at him. "What did you just say?"

"You heard me. I mean, your mom slept with me on the first date; so just imagine how easy she would give it up to any random stranger on the street. Hell, for all anyone knows, she could have lied about him dying because she probably doesn't know who he is." He said and laughed.

My mom became teary-eyed at what Craig just said. I slowly walked over to him and looked him straight in his eyes.

"Is that what you think of my mom? You and I both know that is not the truth, so you better take back what you just said."

"I'm not taking back anything. I speak what's on my mind and that has been on my mind since I met you. You're a bastard and a pain in my ass ever since the first day I saw you."

"That's enough, Craig! You can stand there and talk about me all you want, but do not talk about my son!" my mom yelled.

He went over to her and slapped her across her face. The force was so severe, she fell backwards, nearly hitting her head on the couch.

I punched him, which made him lose his balance.

"That's the last time you put your hands on my mom!"

"Morgan, I can handle this!"

"No; I'm tired of this asshole. In fact, get the hell out!"

"Oh, so you want to be bad right now. You never had a problem spending my money like it's yours."

"I never spent a dime of your money."

"I should be the one telling you to get out. You've been nothing but a damn freeloader."

"You know what, I'll be glad to leave, but my mom is coming with me." I said as I went to take her hand. Craig shoved me away from my mom as I got into his face again.

"Touch me again and I will kill you."

"I would like to see you try."

"I won't go back on my word. I will do it."

Craig leaned into me further as I glanced at him. We knew this day would come, and honestly, I was ready for it.

He tried to strike me, but I threw him down on the ground. I looked at my mom, who had her hands over her mouth, truly afraid for what was happening.

He got up and charged after me. He was trying to push me to the ground, but I was too fast for him. I tripped him, causing him to fall face first onto the couch.

"You punk-ass bitch!" he yelled as he finally was able to push me onto the couch. I dragged him down with me and we both fell on the floor. We began wrestling as my mom was trying to stop us. Craig backhanded her and she fell backwards and hit her head on the table.

I saw the base of his gun poking out of the waistband of his jeans. I was trying to reach for it, when he noticed what I was doing. He knocked my hand away, pushing me onto the floor. His knee was on my throat. He was really trying to kill me.

I used my hands to push his knee off of me and shoved him back onto the ground. We began wrestling again and I was finally able to get the gun. He stared at me as I held it up to his chest.

"Stand up!"

He gave me an evil glance as he slowly got up.

"That's right. Now, you're under my control, you fucking punk! Now, this is what you're going to do. You're going to pack a bag, leave whatever money you have for the mess you have caused and get the fuck out! If you try to contact my mom, I will go to the police and press charges on you."

"And if I don't."

"Then, I'll shoot you point blank where you stand."

He tried to step closer and I aimed it at him.

"Take one more step and I will shoot."

"Morgan, please, just put the gun down!" my mom pleaded. She had her hand on the back of her head. I needed to take her to the hospital, but first, I need this asshole to leave.

"I could always call the cops on you and say you threatened me. I could card you off to juvie, which is where you belong anyways."

He tried to come after me again and the first shot went off. He gave a surprised expression as he glanced from the blood that was spilling from his chest to me. Another shot was fired, hoping I would kill him so he would leave me and my mom alone. No one would miss him if he died. I knew I wouldn't.

My mom was screaming as Craig fell to his knees. I was going to shoot him again when my mom pleaded for me to stop. The gun fell to the floor as I stared at him; he was slowly dying in front of me. My body shook as I watched him struggle to breathe. He began choking on his own blood as he fell forward. A feeling of satisfaction along with fear went through me as he was taking his last breaths. Although I may have possibly killed someone, I wasn't upset over it. I never thought I would take someone's life, but he deserved it.

After seconds of him suffocating from his own spit and blood, he was finally dead. My mom gasped while I went over to the couch. Now, I have to figure out what to do with his body. I surely couldn't leave it here, and my mom was freaking out, so I had to do something.

I pulled out my phone and dialed Lamar's number. He would know what to do.

I stared at Craig's lifeless body. Blood was all over the rug and near my feet as I went over to my mom. I pulled her up from the floor and held her in my arms. I let her sob onto my shoulder while I glanced over at Craig again.

I knew I probably could had avoided what happened. I could have let Craig walk out of here, but I knew how his mind worked. He wouldn't have left, and if he did, he would have come back and made our lives even more miserable. I had to put a stop to him. So honestly, I didn't feel remorseful. Instead, I could actually breathe again....

I slowly opened my eyes and rose up from the bed. I looked around the room, realizing I wasn't in my mom's living room. I looked over and saw Hayley asleep beside me. I let out a slow breath and lay back down. Hayley let out a tiny sigh and opened her eyes. She stared at me with a concerned look.

"Is everything okay?"

I gave her a kiss on the cheek and smiled. "Yeah, everything's cool. Go back to sleep, baby."

She smiled as she looked straight into my eyes. "Well, I'm wide awake now."

"Oh really. So, what do you have in mind?"

She smiled as she got up and straddled me. She leaned down and kissed me. "I can show you better than I can tell you."

I smiled as her tongue slid down my chest. I grabbed her hair as she went to my dick. As soon as her lips touched me, I was gone.

I may have been thinking about that night, but it was definitely a distant memory. I knew I had to think about it eventually, especially once Lamar knows about Hales and I. But the only thing that was on my mind was being pleasured by my girl, which she was doing a damn good job of.

17. Lamar

After having a late-night date with Tamara, I returned back to the house exhausted. I went towards Hayley's room and noticed she wasn't here.

She must be at Paula's. I thought as I went into my room.

I closed the door behind me and went to my bag. I pulled out the camcorder, found some cables, and hooked it to my TV. I turned it on and pressed play on the device. I went to my bed, wondering what I would find regarding Morgan. I prayed that Hayley would not be on this video. If she was, then I basically filmed a sex tape of her, which would be fucking disturbing.

I leaned forward when I saw the two walked into his room. I didn't even know the camera would had been positioned well, but evidentially, it was.

The two went over to the bed when Morgan reached into his pocket. She pulled off his shirt as he did the same for her. I closed my eyes, completely in shock at what I was watching. There was no telling how long they'd been doing this. I didn't know whether to be pissed off or hurt by the two. How could they been doing this behind my back? I guess they thought they were getting away with something, but I had the last laugh.

Before the two started fucking, I turned it off. I wasn't going to watch my sister having sex.

I threw the remote against the wall and put my head in my hands. I wanted to go to Morgan's and punch his ass out, but I wasn't going to. Not now, anyway. I was going to let the two continue thinking their secret was safe until I found the right moment to bust their ass. One way or the other, they would have their secret exposed.

I dialed Tamara's number, wondering if I should tell her, but quickly hung up. I wasn't going to tell her anything because I knew her. She would go run and tell Hayley that I knew, so this one I had to keep to myself.

I picked up my phone again and dialed Hayley's number. I bet she was with that backstabber right now. I hung up when I realized I knew where they were.

I got up from the bed and grabbed my keys. I think I'll go pay them a visit.

***

I went to the place Morgan usually goes to when he wanted to be alone. Much to my surprise, no one was there. I sighed, figuring they had probably left already. I texted him, asking where he was, when he replied, letting me know he was at the diner near his house. I told him I would meet him there. Hayley better not be with him.

Twenty minutes later and I pulled up in the parking lot. Hayley's car wasn't there, so she must have gone home.

I walked into the diner and saw Morgan near the back eating when I pulled up the chair opposite him.

"Hey, what's up?" Morgan asked.

"Nothing. Just wondering what you were up to."

"Nothing, just been here the majority of the night since I didn't want to go back to the house."

"You know you could have spent time at mine."

"I know, but you all are probably tired of me."

"You know you're family, man. You're always welcome."

Morgan gave a tiny smile as he drank his soda. "Thanks. I needed to hear that right now."

"Something happened earlier?"

"Just my mom. She started talking about that night again. I know she can't let go, but I wished she would so I wouldn't have to think about it."

I sighed. Now I couldn't confront him about Hayley. I knew how much that night had affected him, so now; I had to be the friend he needed.

"Can you blame her? She watched her husband get killed right in front of her."

"Are you saying he didn't deserve it?"

"I'm not saying he didn't. He was a straight up asshole and deserved what he got, but that would take a lot out of someone witnessing that."

Morgan hit his fist on the table, which had the people at the nearby booth giving us strange looks.

"Mo, you know you can talk to me anytime about this. I know it's been eating you up and you haven't found a way to let everything go."

"I'm trying Lamar, but I keep wondering will I ever be punished for what happened? I keep thinking that someone will expose me and I could be going off to prison. I can't let that happen."

I glanced at him as he looked out the window. "You know your secret is safe with me."

Morgan nodded. "I know you would never snitch on me, Lamar. You have too much to lose as much as I do."

"You're right. If the situation happened again, I would had done it without any hesitation."

Morgan nodded again. "Thanks, man."

"No problem."

I sighed, knowing what I just said was total bullshit. If I had to protect my sister, I would use that to my advantage, so hopefully whatever they were doing would end soon. If not, then I would have to end it for them.

18. Hayley

It was the day before Thanksgiving, and while everyone was out trying to get last-minute items for their dinners, I was meeting up with Tamara to catch up on some things regarding my brother. Ever since we returned to town, I had this crazy notion that he was slowly learning about Morgan and me. I could be wrong, but I thought we might have slipped up during dinner.

"Hey, Hales." Tamara said as she came over to me and gave me a hug.

"Hey, Tam. Thanks for meeting me."

"No problem. You actually did me a favor. I had to get out of my house."

"What's going on?"

"There's too many family members there. I'm so glad we only see each other once a year."

I laughed. "I know that's right."

"So, why did you want to meet up?"

I gave a concerned look while wringing my hands together. "Has Lamar given you any warnings about Morgan and me?"

She glanced at me and shook her head. "No. Why would you think that?"

"We kind of slipped up at dinner last night."

"What did you two do?"

"Morgan was trying to calm me down since we were all in the same room. Let's just say he took it a little too far."

"Seriously? At the table?"

"It was actually kind of spontaneous."

Tamara rolled her eyes. "I bet. And I'm sure obvious. No one said anything."

"Not a word."

"Wow, you two definitely are wild. If you're wondering if Lamar said anything to me about that, then no, he doesn't know. If he did, I would have been hearing about it for hours and I would have been talking him out of kicking Morgan's ass."

"That's what I was afraid of. He could still know but just waiting for a time to expose us."

Tamara gave a nervous look as she stared at me.

"Do you know something, Tamara?"

"It's nothing. We had a talk about you again and I told him that he should leave you alone."

I sighed and leaned back in my chair. "He's not going to listen, Tamara."

"He might have. I told him that you're a grown woman and you should be able to make your own decisions. He was starting to actually agree with my suggestion, so things might change."

"Please. Lamar has been like that with me since I started dating. He's not going to lighten up anytime soon."

"Have a little faith, Hales. Your brother does have a soft spot, so things may change."

I sighed as I watched Morgan walk in. He looked at me and gave a sexy smile as he came over to me.

"Hey, baby." He said as he leaned down and gave me a passionate kiss. My tongue slowly slipped into his mouth as he held me closer to him. Damn, I wanted him to put me on the table and fuck me right there. That was the effect he had on me. I was always horny for him and he was willing and ready to fulfill whatever desires I had.

We pulled away and looked at Tamara, who was blushing.

"Damn, that was hot."

I smiled while Morgan sat down beside me. "I thought you would have been with Lamar right now." He said to Tamara.

"No. He said he had something to do. Besides, Hayley wanted to catch up and this was an excuse for me to get out of my crazy house for a while. Why are you here?"

"I was in the area and saw Hales' car. I was wondering if you wanted to spend a couple of hours alone before Paula's party."

I smiled as I kissed him. "You know I would."

He leaned over and kissed me again, which made Tamara stand up.

"And that is my cue to leave. Enjoy yourself you two, but somewhere a little more private." She said while giving us a wink.

I waved my hand as Morgan looked at me.

"You know, she's right."

"I guess she is, especially if Lamar sees us."

"At this point, I don't care if he does; I just can't do what I want to you in front of everyone."

My heart started to beat furiously as he took my hand. I threw a $5 dollar bill on the table for my drink and we went to the parking lot. We approached his car, which was near the corner of the restaurant as he leaned my back against the door.

"I want you right now." He said. His dick was on hard against me as he grabbed my ass.

"I know you want me right now too. I bet you're dripping wet, wishing my tongue was between your thighs, your legs wrapped around my shoulders as I taste every single drop of you." He whispered.

He slipped his hand underneath my shirt, caressing my stomach before pushing my bra up to feel my breasts. I moaned against his ear as he unlocked his car. He took me to the backseat as he got in and closed the door. Good thing the windows were tinted; otherwise, I wouldn't be getting ready to fuck in his car.

He took off my shirt and unbuttoned my jeans as I did the same for him. He grabbed a condom from the side compartment as I kissed the side of his neck. I moved my tongue around his outer ear while giving it a slight tug.

He laid me down as he buried his tongue in me, pulling my legs around his shoulders as he began his work on me. Since the backseat was sort of small, the position was uncomfortable, but he was making up for it with the way I was feeling. I pulled his hair, which made him pull on my clit. The sudden reaction made me scream as he put a finger in me. With both movements going through me, I was cumming faster than I wanted to, making me squirt as his tongue continue to fuck me.

He glanced up at me and smiled as he tore open the condom wrapper. He sat down, inserting it on him and pulled me down on him.

"Let's see if you can do that again." He said as he slowly stroked me. I closed my eyes, feeling good from his touch as he bit my earlobe.

"Morgan." I whispered as his hand went down my back, giving me chills throughout my body.

"Say my name again." He said. He hands were going to my ass, which had my body on fire.

He moved my hips, bringing me down on his dick as he leaned his head back. My hands were gripping the seats as we increased our speed.

"You ready to cum, baby?" Morgan asked.

I didn't know why he would say that until he leaned my body back on him. My clit was throbbing as he held my waist. My entire body was growing weak as he kept going in me. I grabbed on to the sides of the drivers and passenger's seats as my legs were moving against him.

"Cum for me, Hayley." He demanded and I was done.

I really hope no one was near the car, because they probably heard me screaming his name. My entire body collapsed as he pulled me back up to face him. He stared at me while he went slower. He grabbed my hair as he continued, whispering in my ear how much he loved me. I held him tighter as tears were streaming down my cheeks. He didn't know how much those words meant to me. When I said I loved him too, that was when I knew he was cumming.

He held me as I buried my face into his neck. He kissed the side of my forehead and sighed.

"We have to figure out a way to tell Lamar. I don't know how much more of this I can do. I want to be able to tell everyone how much I love you. He's going to have to accept that we're together."

I looked at him and he touched my cheek.

"Hayley, you mean so much to me. Even though our relationship started off rocky, just know I will be with you till the end. Lamar will have to tear me away from you with his bare hands if he has to."

"You know it might come to that."

"If it does, then it does. I want to be able to go out with you, go to sleep with you and wake up to you. I want to be able to live with you, and that's something we're not doing right now. I don't want to keep having our life be a damn secret. We should be proud of it and tell everyone about it."

"I know, but Lamar..."

"I know how your brother is. Eventually, he will have to get over it. I'm not going to allow him to break us up."

"Morgan, I want to be able to do all of that and more, but we both know how Lamar can be. He would be even crazier than he already is."

"I don't care, Hales. If he does become that way, just know that I'll be there to fight both of our battles."

"I don't need you to fight my battles."

"I know; that's one of the things I love about you. You never back down from anything. That's a good thing, especially with a brother like Lamar. You need that type of personality to get through him."

"So, what do you want to do?"

"We could always tell him tonight or next week, but regardless, we should do it."

I nodded as he kissed my lips.

"Damn, I could suck on those all day."

"Hmm, what else could you do to me?"

"There's a lot of things I could do. What we just did was a preview."

"Oh really."

"Definitely. Let's go to my place. We can come back and get your car."

I nodded as I put on my jeans. I climbed to the passenger side and Morgan slapped my ass, which made me squeal.

"I couldn't help it."

I smiled as he put on his clothes and got out of the car. Once he got back in, he took my hand and smiled.

"Everything will work out. I can feel it."

I nodded again as he started up the ignition. I really hope he was right, but I was scared as to what Lamar would do. He never was the type to back away from a situation, so this one would not be any different. I just hope he was able to see our way of thinking instead of his and be able to let the two people he cared about actually become a couple. If not, then I would have to put matters into my own hands. If that did happen, trust me, it wouldn't be pretty.

19. Hayley

"Did you bring it?"

I gave Paula an annoyed look and shoved the bag of snacks to her.

"I don't see why you're planning a party tonight. It's the day before Thanksgiving."

"And that's why. We need to have a get-together with all of our friends since we're all back from college."

"And your parents don't care that you're throwing a party?"

"No, they encouraged it."

"Of course." I said as I walked in.

"So, how are things with Morgan?" she asked while putting the bag on the counter.

"Everything is great. Our relationship is perfect."

Paula gave a slight smile and went into the kitchen. "I'm glad he's treating you right, Hales."

"Was there any doubt that he wouldn't?"

"It is Morgan."

"Well, I never doubted him. He's wonderful."

"If you say so." She whispered.

"Do you have a problem with me and Morgan?"

"Why would you think that?"

"I don't know; lately, your attitude has been different around the two of us, as if you're jealous that we're together."

"Seriously, Hayley. If you must know, not every woman wants your man."

"I didn't say every woman did, but you just might."

Paula chuckled. "You're really delusional if you think that. For starters, I don't date white men."

"You don't, but I've seen you checking him out a couple of times. You don't have to lie to me; if you think he's attractive, then say it."

"I don't Hales, so drop it."

I shrugged and she sighed. "Listen, I didn't mean to push your buttons, but I just noticed some things, that's all."

"You don't have to worry; I don't want your man."

"Well, that's good to know."

Paula sighed and threw a straw at me. I threw it back at her and smiled.

"Now, let's get ready for this party, shall we?"

"Fine; lead the way." I said.

A part of me wanted to believe Paula, but I knew she was lying. I just hope I was wrong about my suspicions.

***

After getting the house set-up, it was time to get ready for the party. I walked downstairs wearing a winter white peplum top, black liquid jeggings, and black and gold spiked heels. I checked out my hair in the hall mirror before going to the living room. The party was already going as several of our classmates were centered around the room. I said hi to a couple of people before heading into the kitchen.

"I guess you weren't lying. This party is already going off."

"I know. Had a bigger turnout than I expected. Oh well."

I watched the door open as Morgan, Lamar, and Tamara walked in. He looked at me and smiled.

"So, how are you two going to pull it off tonight?"

I sighed. "Honestly, I don't know."

"Hayley Stevens."

"Tyler Harrison."

He smiled as he came up to me for a hug. His hold was a little tight as he breathed into my hair.

"Wow, you look gorgeous; but you always were."

I blushed as I glanced at him. Besides my little obsession with Morgan, I also had a thing for Tyler. Caramel complexion, light brown eyes and muscular physique, he had all the girls running after him at our high school. The last time I saw him, he had locs, but now his hair was in a short fade. He was too sexy, which had me squeezing my thighs together. That caught me off guard since Morgan was the only man to have me doing that.

"You look great, Tyler."

"Thanks. Sort of did a transformation when I went to college."

"You looked good even before hand."

His eyes scanned my body as he put a hand around my waist. "So, what's been going on with you? It's been awhile since we last saw each other."

"Yeah, it has. Things are going great. I'm doing well with my classes and I'm even looking into doing a couple of internships with party promoters."

"For real? That's cool. You have to invite me to a party then; that's if you can."

"I'll see what I can do. But what about you? What you been up to?"

"Everything's good. I have an early acceptance into law school."

"Really! Wow, that's amazing."

"Yeah, I'm not sure if I'll take it though. Honestly, I don't even know if I still want to pursue being a lawyer."

"Well, that's something you can think about later. You're just a junior."

"Which means I really have to think about it. It'll all come together eventually."

"It definitely will."

"You want to dance?"

I glanced over at Morgan who had a beer in his hand and a curious look on his face. I looked at Tyler and smiled.

"I don't think so."

"Come on, I won't bite, unless you want me to."

I stared at him, not sure what to say after that. Even though Tyler was fine, he was no match to Morgan. I glanced over at him again and he continued to stare at me while drinking his beer. He was wondering what I was going to do. I looked at Tyler again and shook my head.

"Sorry, but no."

"Oh come on, Hales, it's just a dance." Paula said and smiled.

I looked at her, wondering what the hell she was doing. I saw her looking at Morgan, who gave her a dirty look.

She pushed the two of us to the center of the living room. I gave Paula a dirty look of my own as I kept some distance from Tyler and moved side to side. He grabbed my waist and pulled me closer to him, which didn't go too well with Morgan. He was about to come over to us when Tamara pulled him back. I'm not sure where Lamar was, but it was a good thing he wasn't witnessing this.

"Sorry, Tyler, but I'm not in the mood to dance. Maybe next time."

"No problem. Can I get your number, though?"

"No; I have a man."

He nodded. "I kind of figured. Well, it was nice seeing you, Hales."

"You too, Tyler."

He smiled and walked away.

I went over to Paula and grabbed her arm and went to the patio. As soon as we were out of ear shot from everyone, I went in on her.

"What the hell was that?"

"What was what?"

"Don't play dumb with me. You did that on purpose."

"Oh stop it, Hayley. As I mentioned before, I don't want your man."

"You might not, but you're jealous of me being happy."

"You really full of it."

"You were the supportive friend beforehand when you knew I couldn't get with Morgan; but when I finally did, you've have a problem with it. You're jealous."

Paula laughed. "Whatever, get over yourself."

She walked away from me while I shook my head. Maybe Paula wasn't the friend I thought she was.

20. Morgan

I watched as Paula was trying to make Hayley dance with that guy. I knew she was jealous of her. Hayley was finally seeing Paula for who she was; which was something I saw in her for years.

I shook my head and went to find the bathroom. I saw there was a line for the one downstairs. I couldn't wait so I went upstairs. I found the closest one and went inside. After I handled my business, I was washing my hands when the door opened. I turned around and saw Paula walk in, giving me a sweet smile.

"What are you doing?" I asked while giving her a strange look.

"I just wanted to talk to you about Hayley. When I saw you coming up here, I followed you."

"I don't have anything to say to you."

"Come on, Morgan. When are you going to stop this thing you're doing with Hayley? I mean, you got want you wanted, so you can move on."

"What are you talking about? In fact, what were you trying to pull earlier?"

"I was just getting her to dance with a sexy man. Remember, Lamar doesn't know that you two are together, so things have to be as normal as possible."

"You did that to make me jealous. Too bad your plan didn't work." I said as I went to the door. I was trying to open it, but she blocked it and looked at my body.

"I have to admit, you are so sexy."

"What are you doing, Paula?"

"I can be so much better for you than Hayley. You can't even admit you're with her because of her crazy ass brother. At least with me, you wouldn't have to hide us being together."

"That's if I wanted to be with you. I don't, Paula."

"I'll change your mind." She said as she stepped closer to me.

I moved her out of the way to open the door when she turned me around and kissed me. I pushed her off of me and turned to the door. Hayley was standing there glancing at the two of us. I became nervous, hoping she wasn't thinking the worse. Hopefully she would know that I would never want her friend when I was in love with her.

"Hayley..."

"So it is true? I tried to deny it, but my suspicions were confirmed."

I sighed. This didn't look good at all.

"You stupid bitch."

I glanced at Hayley who was staring straight at Paula. She folded her arms across her chest and smirked.

"All this time, I thought you were my friend."

"Awww, are you going to cry, Hales? So, I wanted to fuck your man; big deal."

"I defended you to people when they said how much of a slut you were, but now, I have to agree with them! I can't believe you would try and get with him!"

"Oh please, it's not like you two will be together long. With his roaming eyes and your crazy brother, you two don't stand a chance."

"You don't know that."

"Am I hitting a nerve, because you seem pretty nervous right now? Unless what I'm saying is true."

"Fucking bitch!" Hayley yelled as she went after her. I grabbed her by the waist and pulled her closer to me.

"Stop Hayley, she's not worth it."

"Well, Morgan, if you ever get bored with her, I'm just a phone call away. You may think you love her, but you'll be back to your cheating ways soon."

Hayley tried to pull away from me when Paula walked past us. She shoved her, nearly causing her to fall. I figured that was enough. I let Hayley go as she grabbed her hair and pulled her to face her. She slapped her which led Paula to push her against the wall. The two began wrestling each other when Hayley shoved her to the ground. I don't know how anyone knew what was happening, because now a crowd was forming in the hallway.

Tamara and Lamar pushed their way into the bathroom as I tried to grab Hayley. Before Lamar could get Paula, Hayley decked her across her face, which knocked her to the ground.

"Come after me again, bitch and I'll do a lot worse."

She got up and lunged after her when Lamar held her back.

"I could always tell Lamar what you've been up to."

I wanted to knock her out myself, but I don't hit females; that's why I let Hayley go so she could do it for me.

"What the hell is going on? You two are best friends and you're fighting each other." Lamar said.

Paula laughed as she shrugged from Lamar's grasp. "Why don't you ask your best friend, Lamar? He has a lot to do with why we're fighting."

Lamar glanced at me and sighed. "What is she talking about?"

"She's drunk, Lamar. She doesn't know what she's saying right now."

"I'm not drunk! You and H..."

And that's when Hayley pulled away from me and knocked her unconscious, slumping into Lamar's arms. He looked at her in shock.

"What the hell, Hayley!"

"She deserved it." She said. She pushed past everyone and left the bathroom.

Lamar tried to get my attention, but I ran after Hayley. I pushed past everyone and caught up with her rushing out the door.

"Hayley!"

"What Morgan! Even though she was a bitch, she does have a point."

"What is that? I hope you didn't believe her about me cheating on you."

"You might get bored with me, Morgan. You never been with a female long enough to get to know her. How do I know you won't do that to me too?"

"Hales, don't believe the words she just said. I told you I loved you. I have never told that to any woman before, besides my mom, of course. But I meant what I said with that. I don't take that word lightly, so that means something when I admitted it to you."

She stared at me as I went up to her and put her in my arms, giving her a passionate kiss. I knew I was taking a risk, especially if Lamar saw us, but I didn't care anymore. I was tired of hiding our relationship. I wanted him and everyone to know how special she was to me. If I got my ass kicked for it, so be it.

She pulled apart from me and held the back of my neck.

"Let's go to your place."

I nodded and we headed to our cars. I hoped she would never doubt my love for her, because she was special to me, and I would do everything in my power to protect her.

21. Hayley

We reached his place in record time as we both got out of our cars. He came up to me, putting his hands through my hair and roughly kissed me. My knees were getting weak as he picked me up and took me inside. He closed the door and put my back against the wall. The only light shining was from the outside as he put my feet to the ground. We quickly took off each other's clothes as he reached into his jeans pocket for a condom, which I wish he didn't do. I needed him inside of me now and I couldn't wait for him to put one on.

"I need you now Morgan."

He smiled as he put it on himself. He picked me up while I held onto him. He held my legs, spreading me wide as he pushed himself inside of me. I started to pant from the sensation. Even though he was rough, it still felt good.

"How bad do you want it?" He asked, as he pushed himself in me again. He tried to pull out when I moaned, letting him know how I wanted it.

How he had me positioned made me feel everything, which was a mixture of pain and pleasure. I felt as if I was being spilt in two as my body began to combust. My back was banging against the wall as he pulled me in even further, making me bounce on him. The pressure was building as my legs grew weak and my breath was becoming ragged.

"Shit, I'm cumminnng!" I screamed.

"That's what I want to hear."

My body collapsed as I held onto him. He pulled me down onto the floor as he stared at me. He swept a curl from my face as he slowly stroked me. He was no longer forceful, but gentle, as he kissed my lips. His hand went down my leg as he continued stroking in me, while looking into my eyes.

"You are so beautiful." He said and kissed me again.

I looked at him as we both moved together. As first, we were straight fucking; now, we were making love. I loved both ways, but this was more emotional. The way he looked at me; how he touched me. It showed how much he loved me, just like I loved him.

He held me tight as my body was breaking down again. He gave me a passionate stare while he pull up my leg. His hand went down my thigh, palming my ass before squeezing my cheeks. The sensation was too much as I was cumming again; but this time I wasn't alone. That was another thing I loved about us, because it made the experience even more beautiful.

I had to catch my breath. My legs were still wrapped around him. He slowly touched me, which made me shiver.

"Promise me our relationship will last. That whatever issues we have we can get through them together."

He stared at me and nodded. "I promise, baby."

He held me as I gave a huge sigh. I knew I was asking for too much, but I needed that feeling of hope, even if it was just for a little while.

***

We stayed together for the entire night as we held each other. I knew what happened earlier was still on his mind, just like it was on mine. We both knew the consequences we could face now that Paula could spill our secret. With Brandon, he wasn't an issue, but she was a loose cannon. She could expose us in a heartbeat. But that wasn't the only thing that was bothering me. The idea that I lost my best friend tonight hurt me to the core. We became friends ever since we had the same class in the fourth grade, so it was hard to believe that she would turn on me like that.

Morgan looked at me and kissed my forehead. "It's okay to be upset or sad, baby."

I lowered my head as he put my head on his chest. I could hear his heartbeat as he slowly caressed my shoulder.

"I still can't believe she would do that to me. I have stood by her for so long and defended her when people said things about her. It just amazes me how people can change. Did I do something to her to make her do this to me?"

"You were a good friend to her, so don't feel like this is your fault. She's the type of person that wants attention and will do whatever she can to get it, even if it means hurting the people closest to her."

"We were friends since elementary. She was actually the only real friend I had."

"You know that's not true, right? You have me and Tamara."

"I know, but it's kind of hard knowing that the two of us will no longer be friends again."

He looked ahead at the wall and sighed. "I know how you feel. I feel that way about Lamar and me."

"I need to know what Lamar has on you that kept you away from me. I know he has something on you because you have found every excuse possible not to be with me."

Morgan was speechless to what I just said.

"Why would you think that?"

"I'm not dumb; I know there's something going on. Does it have something to do with the incident you had at 16?"

He didn't answer as he stared at the wall. I pulled his face to mine, making him stare into my eyes.

"Answer me, Morgan. Does my brother know what happened and used it so you couldn't be with me?"

"I'm not going to answer that, Hales."

"Why not? If he's using this against you, then he shouldn't. What happened that made him blackmail you, Morgan?"

"I don't want to talk about this, Hayley."

"Well, you better tell me something, Morgan."

He sighed as he ran a hand through his hair. He glanced at me and sighed again. "Yes, it does have something to do with the incident when I was 16. Yes, he knows about it and used it as leverage so I couldn't be with you; but it's not what you think. He's a part of the incident too."

I glanced at him, wondering what the hell was going on. Why would Lamar use the incident when he was a part of it too?

"That doesn't make sense."

"I said too much. I can't tell you anything else because it's to protect you. The less you know, the better things will be."

"Fine then; if you won't tell me what happened then I'll ask Lamar."

"He won't tell you either. He's trying to protect you as well."

"Morgan..."

"Stop it, Hayley! You do not need to know what happened!"

I rose up from the bed and went to grab my clothes. He cursed under his breath as he got up as well. He came over to me and grabbed my clothes from me.

"Where are you going?"

"If you're not going to be straight with me, then I'm leaving. I can't be with you if you're not honest with me."

"It's to protect you, Hayley!"

"I don't need your protection! I'm so sick and tired of hearing that from you and Lamar. I'm not a little girl, so don't give me that shit about protecting me!"

"But it is! Although I don't regret what I've done, there are people who think I should be punished for it and they're probably still out there. They will do what they can to hurt me just as much as I hurt them."

I stared at Morgan as he ran his hand through his hair again, making it disheveled. His blue eyes became lost and afraid as he took my hands into his.

"Hales, I can't lose you. If I do, I will literally lose my fucking mind, and if I know I'm the reason for anything happening to you, I wouldn't be able to forgive myself."

"Who said that you would lose me? I love you, Morgan, and I would accept whatever you did. Please, just help me understand what led my brother into blackmailing you?"

"I'm sorry, but I can't. Please, just know that it's for your own good that you never knew about it."

I lowered my head when Morgan lifted up my face. He stared at me and bent down to kiss my neck. His lips trailed down to my collarbone and I moaned. I knew I should try and get some sort of information out of him, but he was touching my spot, which had me at a loss for words.

He began kissing my shoulder and I touched the back of his neck. He came back to my face and kissed me, causing me to gasp. Before I knew it, we were laying back on the bed. I knew I needed to find out what happened with him and Lamar, but right now, I needed to feel close to him and be one with him again.

22. Morgan

I knew Hayley would start asking about the incident. I knew she would try and find a way for me to slip up and admit what happened, but I couldn't do it. I couldn't tell her what happened and why Lamar used it to keep me away from her.

So much was going through my head as I stared out at the window. Hayley went to get something to eat for us, which I told her I would go with her, but being the stubborn girl she was, she insisted on going by herself.

I checked my watch when the doorbell rang. I gave a curious look, wondering why she would be ringing the doorbell when I gave her a key.

I went to the door and opened it. To my surprise, Lamar was on the other end, giving me a heated look.

"Hey Lamar. What are you doing here?"

He didn't say anything as he walked inside. I turned to stare at him as I closed the door.

"Is everything okay?"

He turned to stare at me. "Well, I came by to see if everything was okay. Things were kind of tense at Paula's."

"It was. How did you know I was here?"

Lamar glanced at me and smiled. "I figured you had to be since you wasn't at your house."

I didn't like how Lamar was staring at me as he went over to the couch and sat down.

"Everything is cool. After I calmed Hayley down, I left and came here."

"Really, because it looks as if Hayley disappeared at the same time you did. I mean, it wouldn't be unusual since she got into it with Paula, but what had me thinking was why were the three of you upstairs in the first place; and when Paula made that comment about you, it really had me going."

"Where are you getting at, Lamar?"

"Are you fucking my sister?"

I stared at Lamar as he nodded. "I started to get suspicious of you two with the looks you were giving each other on campus and the strange encounters you two had when you're both in the same place at the same time; but what really had me convinced was at dinner when you were finger fucking her underneath the damn table!"

"Lamar..."

"Don't give me that bullshit that you're in love with her! You saw her as a conquest and you went after it. Now that you finally did, I'm sure you'll dump her like all the rest of your women."

"You don't know what you're talking about. For starters, Hayley and I are..."

"Not together? That's not what I heard."

"Listen, if Paula told you..."

"Paula didn't tell me a damn thing! I heard from yours and Hayley's own damn mouths!"

He reached into his jeans pocket and threw something at me. I looked at it and saw that it was his phone. I glanced at him with a confused look while he was still giving me a heated one.

"Press play on the video."

I sighed and did what he asked. I shook my head at what I was seeing.

"You recorded Hayley and I having sex? Are you crazy?!" I exclaimed while throwing the phone on the couch.

"I told you I would do what I needed to protect her. You're my boy and all but you don't deserve her."

"No man deserve her in your eyes. I love Hayley and I'll do whatever I can to protect her."

"Don't give me that. You love to play the field; you'll eventually get tired of her and move on and I'll have to be the one to pick up the pieces."

"Don't you think I was that way because I couldn't be with Hayley? She was the one I wanted but since we made that pact I kept my distance from her."

"Which didn't work."

"I was tired of pretending, Lamar! I love your sister! What is wrong with that?!"

"Just stay away from her." Lamar said while getting up.

"No, I'm not. I'm going to continue seeing her and being with her. The truth is out now, so it's nothing you can do about it."

"Oh really? What if I expose your damn secret and you'll be going to prison."

"Go ahead, but I guess you'll be in a cell with me."

"I might, but I'll receive less time if I ask for a plea bargain."

I glanced at him. "So you're willing to turn me over because of your stupid jealousy? I swear you act like a fucking ex instead of her brother!"

Lamar came up to me and shoved me. "You want to go there, then let's go there. I don't want you around her because she deserves better than some fucking white trash!"

I stared at him. I couldn't believe he was saying that to me. We were friends since kindergarten. We were like brothers and this is what he thought of me?

"What did you say?"

"You heard me. If you think you're going to keep being with her, then you have another thing coming."

I shoved him and he fell backwards onto the couch. "After everything we have been through and this is how you treat me? Because I'm in love with your sister!"

"She won't be in love with you after what I have to tell her. That you killed your stepfather and burned his body to a crisp. You know what I could do with that information. That would make her stay away from you."

"Well, I guess you'll be joining me then, since you helped me burn his body! You know why I had to kill him."

"I know, but to keep you away from my sister, I will use that against you."

I sighed. If he wanted to play dirty, then that was fine by me.

"In fact, why don't I call the police now, so they can arrest you? I can always say that you forced me to do it, so I'll get off for it."

"Son of a bitch."

He gave me an evil smile as he grabbed his phone from the couch. I wasn't going to let him take me down. I went over to him and knocked the phone out of his hand. He tried to punch me, but I was too quick. I decked him across his jaw, pulling him down onto the floor. He pushed me off of him and grabbed my neck. I began choking as he threw me down. I released myself from his hold and held him down on the ground. All of a sudden, I snapped and I begin to repeatedly hit him. I couldn't stop as blood began to fly from his mouth and nose. I was trying to get him to go unconscious, which was fine by me, with the shit he had just said.

I heard the door fly open and the sound of Hayley screaming. I continued going when she tried to take me away from Lamar.

"Morgan, baby, stop!"

I struggled from Hayley's grasp as she tightly held onto me.

I didn't even notice Tamara had come in as she went over to Lamar. She began yelling to see if he was conscious. She checked his pulse and sighed.

"His pulse is weak, but he's still alive. I need to call 911."

I went over to the door and slid down onto the floor. I watched as Tamara was on the phone

talking to the operator. Hayley came in front of me and stared into my eyes.

"What happened? What did you do?"

I continued staring at Lamar unconscious on the floor. Is this what our friendship had come to?

Him belittling me and me nearly killing him? What happened to when everything was simple with us? When we used to play with our toys and shoot hoops and played video games. I guess life happened.

Tamara came over to us and looked at me. "What in the hell happened, Morgan? I knew things

would have been bad, but..."

"I'm sorry. Things got a little heated and I had to defend myself."

Hayley looked at me and she began to cry. I closed my eyes, knowing that I caused this. I knew I

would do this. The one thing I tried to avoid; I ended up doing and that was hurt her.

I slowly got up and went to the door. I glanced at Lamar's body again before heading to the garage.

"Morgan! Morgan, please don't leave!" Hayley yelled.

I walked in where my motorcycle was parked.

"Morgan!"

I turned and saw Hayley staring at me.

"Stay with your brother, Hayley."

"I need to be with you."

"Please, Hayley. Lamar's right. I'm not any good for you."

She climbed on the back of the bike and wrapped her arms around my waist.

"Wherever you going to, I want to be there with you."

"But Lamar..."

"Tamara's with him. I'll check on him later, but first, I need to check on you, I know he pushed your buttons and you reacted. But let's go before the ambulance and the police comes."

"The police..."

"They were dispatched because it was an assault, Morgan."

"Did Tamara..."

"She didn't say that you did it. She said she found him laying on the floor when she arrived."

I sighed. This made me think about that night, which only made me upset.

"We need to go, Morgan."

I started up the bike and Hayley held me tighter. I drove out of the garage and into the dark night.

23. Hayley

I lay my head on Morgan's back as he drove. He'd been driving for nearly an hour now and I didn't have a clue to where he was going. I looked at the road ahead and sighed. How in the hell did I get into this mess? One minute, I was happy and in love; now, I was scared because I didn't know what this would mean for the two of us. I should have been with my brother to see if he was okay, but I couldn't. I knew he pushed Morgan to the brink. I knew Lamar would do this, that's why I wanted things to be kept a secret. If I find out that Paula had something to do with this, I would definitely beat her ass for sure.

Morgan turned into a motel parking lot and turned off the bike. He got off and helped me off. While he went to talk to the clerk, I stood outside and took in the view around me. I sighed, wondering if this is where he would spend the rest of his time or would he up and go back to school or out of the state. So much was probably going through his mind right now, that's why I had to be with him so he would rationally think about his choices.

He came up to me and smiled. "If you need a change of clothes or a toothbrush, I could always go to the store that we saw on our way here."

"I'm okay for now."

He nodded and he took my hand to go to our room. He used the key card to grant access and we walked in. It was a typical motel room, with the tacky looking couch at the front entrance. A desk was in the corner with a flat screen TV mounted on the wall. The bed looked okay, but the comforter had seen better days. I sighed as I went over to sit down.

"Are you hungry? I know you were going out for food, but..."

"I lost my appetite, but thanks."

He sat down beside me and looked straight into my eyes.

"I think I owe you an explanation now."

"It would be nice."

"Lamar came by the house clearly pissed about us. He confronted me about it, saying I didn't deserve to be with you."

"But how did he know? Did Paula say something?"

"No. He recorded us having sex, Hales."

I stared at the wall, clearly pissed at what he'd done. Maybe it's good he's already in the hospital, because I probably would have put him there myself.

"Wow, that's an invasion of privacy. How was he able to record us?"

"I don't know; all I know it was on his phone. Anyway, he belittled me, calling me white trash and that's when I snapped."

"I'm so sorry, Morgan."

"That wasn't the only reason, though. He was going to turn me into the police for what I'd done. I had to stop him, so I started hitting him. He was choking me, so I had to defend myself. Other than that, I wouldn't had done what I did."

"Are you ready to tell me what happened?"

He took a deep breath and grabbed my hand. I put it up to his cheek as he held onto it.

"That day when I was 16, it was my mom's birthday, and she had set-up this great evening with Craig since she wanted him to help celebrate it. She had asked me to help set-up everything, which I didn't want to do, but I figured it was her birthday, I didn't want any issues to occur.

"Once everything was done, he came home, saw everything and completely flipped. He told her he was tired and wasn't going to do anything with her. He told her to go into the kitchen and fix his dinner and the smile on his face would be her birthday present. While that made my mom cry, it pissed me off; with all the shit he had put her through, she was in love with him, and that set me off.

"I confronted him, telling him it was her birthday and to at least try and do something for her. He said was doing enough by giving us a roof over our heads and food to eat. He went on to say he didn't have to do a damn thing for me since I wasn't his. That was when my mom got upset. She went after him, telling him how could he be so cruel to me. Like he cared if he was. He didn't like me just like I didn't like him."

"He continued on, saying how much of a slut my mom was and that she probably lied about my dad dying because she probably didn't know who he was with all the whoring around she was doing. When he said that, something inside of me snapped and I went off on him. Before I knew it, the two of us were arguing when I saw his gun. I knew he had one because in his own words he had to protect himself from anyone and everyone. We fought for a bit until I was able to get his gun. I pointed it at him, telling him to get his shit and leave. After he tried to come after me, I shot him point blank in the chest."

"Oh Morgan."

"That wasn't the end of it. After I shot him, I didn't know what to do. I was scared because I had just killed someone, even if he did deserve it. My mom was in a panic, so she wasn't able to help me, so I called Lamar to help. He came over and we tried to figure out a way to get rid of him so it wouldn't trace back to me. Lamar was the one who thought of burning his body."

"So there wouldn't be any evidence." I whispered.

"I didn't want to do it at first, but I had to. Even though it was self-defense, I still would have been arrested and charged, so I had to do it. Lamar and I rolled up his body in a rug, carried him to an open field near the park and we burned his body."

"Wow."

"Lamar felt this was perfect for him to use against me. He knew I had a thing for you and he

tried everything he could to not have us together, so he told me since he'd helped me cover up

the murder that I had to stay away from you. I couldn't get involved with you nor try anything

with you. You were off-limits."

"But that wasn't his decision to make. And to use something like that against you was truly

terrible. I can't believe he did that."

"I went along with it because he could turn me in, but honestly, he could have been going to

prison too for being an accessory to murder, which I mentioned; but he figured he wasn't the one who killed him, so he probably could have gotten off."

"But he helped burn his body; he had as much to do with the murder as you did."

"Anyway, I agreed to it, knowing how much this had destroyed my mom. She hasn't been the

same since that night."

"I can imagine."

"As for me, I've just been going through the motions, wondering if anyone knew what happened.

He had family members and they came by the house and called wondering if we had seen him.

That was when they filed a missing person report on him, which to this day, they still have never

found a body."

"So why do you think someone may be after you?"

"Because more likely his family knows my mom and I had something to do with his

disappearance. Well, more me than my mom. Craig showed his hatred for me to his family, so

they figured I had some part of him suddenly vanishing. They know people in high places, so it's

a possibility they have been following me without me even knowing.

"That's why I didn't want to get involved with you, because I knew how much trouble I would bring in your life. Now I can't rely on the one person who has helped me with everything, so

now, I'm alone."

I held his hand and smiled. "No, you're not."

"Hales, I don't want you to go against your family for me."

"I know, but Lamar was wrong for what happened. Do I condone what you did? No, but I can

understand why you did it. Lamar went too far and he knew what could happen if something like

this occurred."

"Hales, I don't want you involved in this. You know too much now."

"Which I'm glad you were able to confide in me with. Don't you think if someone is after you that I should be with you?"

Morgan sighed. "I was thinking that."

"Listen, I know that took a lot out of you and I appreciate that. Just know that it wasn't your fault with what happened. You had to do what you felt was right for the situation."

"I know. I understand if you need to see Lamar."

"I'll call Tamara and get an update. I'm going to stay with you. Just know that no matter how much you're trying for me to, I'm not leaving you."

He leaned over and kissed me, which I gladly returned. I know what Morgan did was wrong, but Lamar was also wrong in the situation. I would have to figure out what was best for everyone later; but right now, I needed to keep a close eye on my man so he wouldn't have a relapse as to what happened.

"What about your parents? I'm pretty sure they have been trying to call you."

"I'll just say I couldn't get to my phone. Trust me, I'll make sure and see if he's okay."

I looked at Morgan while he stared at the TV. "If you think his family is after you, wouldn't they had checked one of his properties or even the house to do something?"

"That's the issue I'm having. After they filed the report, I haven't heard from them again. They know I'm onto them, that's why they haven't made a move. I know eventually they're waiting on me to slip up; that's why I need to stay on top of everything so I won't."

"I won't let that happen." I said as I held his hand. He pulled me to him as he gave a long sigh.

"I love you, Hayley."

"I love you too, Morgan."

Now that he told me his secret, it would be a tough road ahead for us, but I think we're both ready for what we might face.

***

After an hour of lying beside each other, we both fell asleep. Three hours later and I woke up needing to pee. I slowly got out of Morgan's embrace and walked towards the bathroom.

After I finished, I went to the sink to wash my hands. I stared at myself in the mirror, realizing how horrible I looked. Well, I guess I could give myself a pass after everything that has

happened lately.

I walked back into the room and saw my phone lighting up. I went to it and it was Tamara.

"Hey."

"Hey Hales. I just wanted to let you know Lamar is awake now and he's asking for you."

"If it's about Morgan, I already know, so he doesn't have to use his scare tactics on me, because it's not going to work."

"I don't know what's going on with that, but he wants to press charges on Morgan. The police are here now taking his statement. They plan on bringing him in for questioning. So if you two are still in town, you might want to leave."

I glanced at Morgan who was still asleep. I turned and looked at the window and sighed.

"Why is he pressing charges?"

"He felt he was attacked, which I'm sure he did something to provoke Morgan."

"He did. He told me everything."

"I knew it."

"Why are you helping Morgan? I mean, I'm glad you are, but he put your boyfriend in the hospital."

"Just like you're helping him. He put your brother in the hospital, so you should be more upset, but we both know that Lamar is a hot head and eventually, something was going to happen."

"That's so true."

"But please, just go ahead and go. And honestly, I wouldn't recommend for Morgan to go back to school, because they will try there too."

I sighed. Morgan only had one more semester of college left. Lamar would rather for him to lose everything to heal his bruised ego? Jackass!

"If you want, I could come by wherever you are to bring some clothes for the both of you."

I glanced around wondering if that was a ploy to know where we were. I wasn't going to give her any information.

"That's okay, Tam; we're straight."

"You sure; I..."

"That's okay, Tam. And tell Lamar nice try." I said and hung up.

Now, I'm going to have to change my number.

I went to the bed and lay beside Morgan. He woke up and stared at me.

"What's wrong?"

"Tamara called saying Lamar is going to press charges on you."

"What? That's bullshit and he knows it."

"She told me to warn you so you could leave town. She was even willing to bring us our clothes, but I think she really was trying to figure out where we were."

"Damn. I'm really sorry Hales."

"Stop apologizing. You didn't do anything wrong. We just have to figure out a way to skip town without anyone knowing."

"That's fine, but you're not going."

I gave him a surprised look while he got up. "What?"

"Hayley, you're not the one who needs to run; I do since I'm about to have an arrest warrant. I can't have you following me to places when I don't even know where I'm heading."

"But wouldn't you need me with you if I'm a potential target now?"

"Maybe, but you have your parents here. And even though I want to hit your brother again for this shit, you know he would protect you to the end."

"I don't want his protection, especially with what he's doing."

"Well, you might have to now."

"Morgan…"

"Hales, please, I need you to stay here. I don't want to worry about you if you're with me. I could be putting you in even more danger."

I glanced at him as he gave me a huge hug.

"We were just starting our relationship and now you want to end it?"

"You know I don't, but I love you too much for anything to happen to you."

I wanted to argue, but he was right. It probably was best if I did stayed.

He picked up his keys and jacket. He walked over to me and grabbed my waist and smiled.

"Besides, I'm sure once everything is under control that we'll be together. When that time comes, we wouldn't have to hide our relationship."

"That will be nice."

He gave me a passionate kiss that left me breathless. He pulled away as he pulled out his wallet. He handed me four $20 bills.

"That should cover a cab back."

"Thanks, I guess."

He leaned into me again and gave me another kiss. He slowly touched my hair and smiled.

"I'm going to miss of all this with you. Your hair, your lips. You were always something I looked forward to each and every day. You kept me going because even when everyone else

doubted me, you never did. For that, I have to say thank you. Thank you for being you and the

time that you have graced my life. Just know that I love you and once all of this blows over, I

will come back to you. I have to so we can live the life we both deserve."

I looked away from him as he cupped my chin. "Please, don't do this. This is hard for me too."

"Morgan, I'm willing to go with you. My brother is being an ass and honestly, there's nothing left for me here. I can always finish school online so that wouldn't be an issue."

"That's not the issue with me. I need you to be protected and I can't do that if I'm on the road because of your damn brother."

"Well, I suggest you find a way, because I'm not staying. I understand you want to protect me, but if you love me like you say you do, then you would support me on my decision. I'm not letting you be out there alone. I'm going to be with you every step of the way. I'm going to be there and ride with you, so you're not getting rid of me that easily."

Morgan looked at me and laughed. "You were always a stubborn woman, but that's one of the reasons why I love you."

"So, what do you say? Am I coming with you?"

"Okay."

"I knew I could change your mind."

"I bet. I should put you over my knee and spank you for being so bad."

"That wouldn't be a punishment."

"You little freak. I love that about you too."

I smiled as I put my arms around him. "We'll in this together. I'm going to ride with you until the wheels fall off, so don't expect me to go anywhere."

He turned me around so my back was facing the bed.

"Well, I think I know a place we can go, but you sure you don't want to take anything with you?"

"I can, but I'll have to sneak on campus in case Lamar have anyone looking for you."

"Actually, let's not. We can just start over. There's somewhere I need to go first before we head out."

"Okay."

He stroked my hair and gave me a serious look. "I really hope I'm making a good decision. I don't want to ruin your life over this."

"You won't. Everything will blow over later."

"Let's hope. We better go."

"Where are we going?"

"My uncle's. He stays in Dallas, though."

"You're going to ride your bike all the way to Dallas?"

"Probably won't, but I do want to take it with me. We'll figure that out once we get on the road. But there is one thing I need you to do."

"What's that?"

"Call your mom. She needs to know what happened as well as where you're going. She doesn't need to be worried about you too."

"I'll call her if you do the same for yours."

"I will, once we're on the road. Now, we need to make that stop before we head to Dallas."

I nodded and followed Morgan out of the room. This was going to be interesting, but at least we were still together.

24. Morgan

After leaving the motel, we headed to the stop I needed to make, which was the bank. I had to ask the owner to open it up for me so I could go into my safe deposit box. No owner would graciously open up the bank after hours for any customer; no, the owner was a friend of my dad's and he was the only one who knew about the safe deposit box.

"So, what brings you by, Morgan?" James asked while opening up the safe.

"I need to head out of town unexpectedly and needed some of my belongings."

"Oh, okay. Well you know I would do anything for you since you're Randy's son. How's your mom doing?"

"She's fine."

James nodded and took out the box. "Take your time; I'll just be outside."

"Okay. Thanks, James."

He nodded and went out to the hall.

Hayley glanced at me while I went through my belongings. From my passport to over $20,000 in cash, I took out everything, figuring it was all we needed for our destination.

"This was your dad's box?"

"Yeah. He left it for me after he died. I used it every now and then to keep things hidden. I might also take his car instead of riding the bike."

"What are you going to about that?"

"I might have to leave it behind, but I'll see if my uncle can come and get it. I'm sure he would love to see it anyway since him and my dad fought over it when they were younger."

"I'm sure there's more to the story."

"Of course, which I'll tell you another day. Right now, we have to leave."

Once I grabbed the keys to my dad's Mustang, I thanked James again before heading to the parking lot. Hayley and I got into the car and I smiled. I couldn't believe I still remember the car. Besides his bike, this car was his pride and joy. That's why I never drove it, because I wanted to keep it the way he remembered it.

"You ready to see how our lives are going to be?"

Hayley took my hand and smiled. "Yeah."

I smiled and turned on the ignition. I backed out of the parking spot and headed back on the road.

Wherever it lead us to, I was just glad Hayley was with me. Even though I should had told her to

stay, I couldn't do it. The selfish part of me wanted her with me, so I would have to do

everything within me to keep her safe.

I glanced through my side mirror and saw a car parked near the far end of the lot. I noticed that

car had not moved since we've been here. Honestly, there shouldn't been anyone else here since the bank was closed. Now that I had been driving for about a block now, the car was close behind, trying to figure out where I was going.

I wasn't sure if the car was actually following me. It could just be someone going the same way as me. If they were, I wasn't sure if it was someone from Craig's family or someone Lamar hired, but whoever it was, I knew the time would come when I would finally have to face what I had done. I knew I couldn't continue living my life knowing what I had done. I wasn't going to be obvious to Hayley because that would make her nervous, so I made a left turn to lose the car.

The car was still close behind, going into the same lanes as me as I cut off someone in front of me. I looked through my rearview mirror, trying to see if it was someone I knew; but it was a random stranger.

Hayley glanced behind her as I quickly turned her around.

"Don't look back, he'll know."

She gave a nervous look out of the corner of her eye as I sped up. I cut off another car in front of me as I went on the freeway.

This is not how I wanted her to live her life. I didn't want her to be on guard running because of my actions. Hell, we haven't even left the city yet and someone already chasing us; but we knew it would happen.

The car was still going after us when they grazed our bumper. Hayley gave a nervous look as the car gave another bump, but this time it was harder, as I almost hit the car in front of me. Luckily the car switched to another lane, leading me to also switch over.

"Is someone following us, Morgan?!" Hayley yelled.

I exited off of the freeway, making the other car do the same. I went into the nearest parking lot of a strip center and stopped. If I was going to confront the person who was following us, it might as well be in a public area.

Hayley looked at me as if I was crazy as I got out of the car. She unbuckled her seatbelt when I stopped her.

"Stay in the car."

"No."

"Don't argue with me, Hayley!"

She looked away from me as I got out of the car. I stood at the back bumper as I waited for the person to get out. If he wanted to confront me, he better get out of the car to do it.

I folded my arms across my chest as the person walked toward me. I glanced at him, waiting for whatever he was about to do.

"Who are you and what the hell do you want?"

"You don't need to know who I am, but I know you very well Mr. Carter." The guy said.

"Who sent you to follow me?"

"Can't tell you that either. All I know is I need the girl."

I shook my head, knowing that Lamar was the one who hired this idiot.

"Oh really?"

"Yes. Hand her over and all the charges will be dropped against you."

"I see Lamar didn't waste any time. How did he find me?"

"Just hand Miss Stevens over."

"Give this message to the person who hired you. Fuck you." I said.

"Fine; since you're not cooperating, he gave me another order to do." He said as he pulled out a gun from the waist of his pants.

"Now, hand her over; if you don't I will kill you."

"Well, I guess you're going to have to kill me, then." I said.

The guy was about to come over to me, when I went over to him. I threw him against the car, causing the gun to knock out of his hand. He pushed my face to the side, trying to push me off of him when I threw him on the trunk. He kicked me, throwing me backwards as he went to get the gun. I went after him, slamming him on the pavement as we struggled for the gun. He reached for it, trying to aim it at my chest when I heard a shot go off. The guy fell on me as I looked over. Hayley was standing over us, with a gun in her hand. She was shaking as she glanced from the guy to me.

"Hayley…"

She stared at me, not knowing what to do as she dropped the gun onto the pavement. She put her hand over her mouth as she backed away from us.

I pushed the guy off of me and went over to her. I held her as she began to cry.

"I had to do it. He was going to kill you, so I had to do it."

"It's okay, baby."

"I found the gun under the seat. I didn't even know it was loaded. I was taking a chance when I was aiming it…"

"It's okay."

She was still shaking as I held her even tighter. I didn't want to stay where we were for too long. No one was outside, which was surprising since we were in a shopping center.

"We have to go, baby. Just get in the car."

She nodded and slowly went to the passenger side.

I went inside the guy's car to look for something to wipe Hayley's prints. I found a towel that was in the backseat and wiped down the gun. I threw it in the passenger seat. I went over to the guy and dragged him to his car. I put him in the driver's seat, took the towel again and put the gun in his hand, hoping it looked obvious as a suicide.

I noticed his wallet was inside the console. I took the towel and looked through it. I saw a picture of him along with Craig standing side by side. Now I knew who hired him. I closed the door and ran over to the car.

I looked over at Hayley, who was still in shock. I looked at my hands, seeing if I had any blood on me, which luckily I didn't.

I gave a silent prayer, hoping no one saw what happened. If they did, then we were screwed; but for now, we had to continue.

I started off the car, knowing eventually we would have to ditch it. I didn't want to, but in case someone did see us, they wouldn't be able to ID us.

SOMETHING JUST AIN'T RIGHT

I knew I was going to have to confront what happened, but I wasn't going to do it without a fight. I was wondering when someone was going to make their move; that's why I've been figuring out ways to end this shit so I could live my life. Not only mine now, but Hayley's. She was a part of this as I was, which didn't sit well with me, but it was nothing I could do about it now but protect her.

Now that they decided to start something, I knew that I would have to be waiting and ready for them.

25. Hayley

I stared ahead at the dark road as Morgan continued driving. I couldn't believe what happened. I had just killed someone. I never imagined I would ever do that in my life, but I had to do it. I was protecting Morgan, so it was self-defense. He would had done the same for me, so I shouldn't have felt too guilty about doing it, but I did.

So many things were going through my mind, like whether he was married or had children. If he did, I took someone's father away. Now, I felt sick.

I looked over at Morgan as he gave me an apologetic look. He pulled over onto the side of the road and gave me a hug.

"I'm really sorry. This is why I didn't want to get involved with you. I knew I would mess up your life."

"Morgan, stop."

"No; you're involved in my stupid shit and now, you're not able to walk away. You should have stay behind and let me dealt with whatever was coming my way."

"Morgan, I said I would be with you no matter what. Yes, what I did will bother me possibly for the rest of my life, but I did it to protect you. If I had to do it all over again, I would."

He shook his head and sighed. "At first, I thought Lamar hired the guy to follow us. He kept saying to hand you over and the charges would be dropped. When I was putting him in the car, I looked into his wallet and saw that he knew Craig."

"What? If he knew Craig, then how would he know about Lamar and the charges?"

"I don't know. He could have been lurking around the hospital and used it to his advantage. Whatever the reason, just know that his family and your brother is after me, so I really have to lay low."

"Does your uncle know we're coming?"

"I haven't had the chance to tell him. I'll drive further out of the city before I do."

"What's going to happen, Morgan? I mean, now that this has happened, I could be arrested as well. I never thought I would be thinking about a criminal record or going to jail or..."

"Hayley, everything is going to be okay. Don't worry about what will happen because for all we know, it probably won't get to that point. Right now, we just need to focus on getting to my uncle's without any other issues occurring."

I nodded and continued looking at the road. My phone started to ring. I sighed, realizing I should had changed my number sooner, but with everything that had happened, I hadn't had a chance to. I looked at it and saw my mom's name flashing across the screen. Morgan glanced at me and back at the road.

"You probably need to answer that; after that, you have to either change your number or get a new phone."

I continued to stare at it, not knowing if I should. What if they have someone tracing my phone? I couldn't take that risk.

I saw a gas station while going down the road and pulled on Morgan's arm. "Stop the car!"

He quickly hit the brakes and we both shifted in the seat. He gave me a crazed look as I unbuckled my seat belt.

"What the hell, Hayley?"

"I'm not going to answer my phone, so I'm going to use a pay phone. You have any change?"

He dug into his pocket and took out a few coins. Hopefully this was enough to use it.

We both got out of the car and I went to the pay phone near the station. I checked the change, glad that it was the amount needed, and put it into the slot. I dialed my mom's cell number and waited for a response. Hopefully she would answer since the number would be unfamiliar.

"Hello."

"Mom."

"Hales," she whispered.

"Hi. I know you just called, but I couldn't answer my phone. Are you somewhere private?"

"I'm actually at home. I came back to get a change of clothes. Where are you?"

"I can't say. Are you alone?"

"Yes; your dad is still at the hospital. We've been worried about you, especially since you haven't come to the hospital."

"I know and I'm sorry, but I won't be coming."

"Are you with Morgan?"

"I'm not going to answer that."

"Hales, if you think I'm going to tell Lamar, I'm not. Tamara told me what happened."

"Yes, and I'm sure she's helping him trying to locate me."

"I know she called, but it wasn't for Lamar. It was for me, sweetie. We all knew Lamar was going to start some mess, that's why I wanted you to tell him yourself so it would have softened the blow."

"How was that possible? He would have done the same things that he did when he confronted Morgan. He recorded us having sex, Mom."

"I know. Tamara told me that, too. I know Lamar can be a bit overdramatic sometimes, but he thought he was doing it so you wouldn't be hurt again."

"Hurt again. What are you talking about?"

I could hear my mom sigh as I waited for her to respond. What is going on?

"Sweetie, Lamar has been acting this way because of something that happened years ago with your cousin, Samantha."

I gave a confused look, even though my mom couldn't see me. Why was she bringing up Samantha? She was about the same age as Lamar and the two were close. She used to come by the house all of the time and was pretty cool. She passed away about four years ago, but no one ever mentioned the cause of her death.

"You remembered when her and Lamar were supposed to had went on a trip together but didn't."

"Yeah, because that was the day she died."

"She was heading to the house when she called Lamar, letting him know she had to stop off by her friend's house to get his camcorder. He asked her if she wanted him to go with her, but she declined. When she did, they talked and when she was leaving he tried to kiss her. Samantha always told Lamar that this guy had feelings for her, but she never returned them. She only saw him as a friend, but he thought differently.

"When she told him to stop, he became a different person, telling her she led him on, which she never did. He became even more upset; he took her into his room and repeatedly raped her. After everything, she tried to run when he was asleep. She made it down to a park near his house. When she thought she was clear, she tried to call Lamar to tell him what happened; that was when the guy snatched the phone away, raped her again and then killed her. Her body was discovered in the park by a jogger during his morning run."

A tear fell down my cheek as I heard the story, Now, everything sort of made sense about Lamar's behavior. He felt it was his fault what happened to Samantha; that's why he was trying so hard for me not to be with anyone. Although he was always protective, he became even more after my 16th birthday, which was also around the time Samantha was murdered.

"Wow, Mom, I didn't..."

"I know, sweetie. We didn't want you to know about that, since it hit so close to home. We all wanted to protect you, because we felt that could happen to you; but Lamar became a little over the edge with it, and for that, your father and I are really sorry."

"It's not your fault for what happened."

"We could have done something to stop Lamar."

"Maybe so, but Lamar is his own person. The times when you both tried to talk to him, he wouldn't listen, so his mind was made up."

My mom sighed again into the phone and I looked at Morgan, who had a concerned look.

"How did you all know what happened with Samantha?"

"The guy confessed to everything. He gave details to what happened and even told the police where he dumped her body. He felt guilty about everything and felt he had to come clean."

I closed my eyes, trying to fight back tears. This was all becoming too much.

"I know I shouldn't have told you this, but I figured you needed to know."

"I'm glad you did."

"But Hales, you need to come home. Your dad and Lamar are worried. And trust me, he will not press charges on Morgan. He was just upset and didn't know what else to do to bring you back. He knew if he did, Morgan would have told you to stay, but to everyone's surprise, you left with him."

"How do I know when I return that he still won't?"

"He won't. Your dad talked him out of it."

"Did he tell you all anything else?"

"About what?"

I sighed. If he didn't, I sure wouldn't.

"Nothing. But I can't, not now. Until everything cools down, then I can probably return."

"Hayley..."

"Sorry, Mom, but I can't. I have to be with Morgan. There's more to the story and Morgan can't be there. I'll try to contact you again soon; but just know that I'm okay."

"Hayley, please don't hang up..."

I put the phone back onto the cradle and wiped the tear that fell on my cheek. I turned to stare at Morgan who gave me a hug.

"So he's not pressing charges?"

"No; my parents talked him out of it, even though that was surprising; but he probably figured he was asking for it, too."

"Even if he was, I shouldn't have went there. I should have kept my temper in check."

"So now I know why he's had a problem with me dating. It was all because of our cousin, Samantha. He didn't want what happened to her happen to me."

"I kind of heard some of the conversation. Even he never told me what happened. I'm really sorry."

I nodded and wiped another tear. "We'd better go."

"Okay. Probably in the next hour we could stop somewhere and get something to eat. I'm sure you're starving by now."

"Not really. I'm more exhausted then anything."

"Well, we could get a room and rest."

"You think that's a good idea?"

"We're going to have to eventually."

"Okay."

We both went to the car, knowing we should continue our journey. Now, I had a little understanding to Lamar's behavior throughout the years, but it still didn't excuse what he put me through. I just hope he could find it in his heart that it wasn't his fault for what happened and that he could try and move on with his life.

26. Morgan

After another hour drive, it was time to stop at the nearest motel. As soon as we entered the room, Hayley went straight to the bed to rest. I laid beside her in bed, watching her sleep as I put my hand down her back. I sighed, realizing how much damage I had caused for the both of us. She didn't deserve to be involved in this. Now that she killed someone, she was just as guilty as I was. Honestly, Lamar deserved to kick my ass now for what I'd done to her.

I pulled out my phone from my pocket and dialed my mom's number. I knew I was taking a risk now with calling her, but I knew she wouldn't answer the phone if it was from another number.

After several attempts, I was going to hang up, when she answered.

"Morgan."

"Hi, Mom."

"Where are you? You haven't returned home and I was worried about you."

"Please don't be, but I had to leave and I'm not sure when I'll be back."

"Did you go back to school?"

"No. Actually, I probably won't be returning there either."

"What? What is going on, Morgan?"

"I kind of ran into a little bit of trouble, Mom."

"Does this have something to do with Craig? I knew this was going to happen! This is all my fault!"

"Mom, please don't blame yourself."

"But it is my fault! I married him and you were protecting me. After what happened, I haven't been much help to you and you had to do everything on your own. For that, I'm sorry. I'm so sorry." My mom said as she started to cry.

I glanced at Hayley and sighed. At this point, I wanted to break down myself. Everything was happening too fast and now, I didn't know what else to do. But I knew I couldn't. I had to be strong, not just for myself, but for Hales too.

"Please, Mom, stop crying. Just know that I'm okay. I'm going to beat this, so you don't have to worry about me."

"How can I not. You're my son, Morgan. We took care of each other throughout the years, so it's hard not to worry about you and not knowing where you are."

"You know I'm a fighter. I'm going to get through this."

"I really hope so. And why is Lamar not helping you through this? The two of you were so close, but now, I noticed things have changed. Does it have to do with you being with Hayley?"

I sighed. I really didn't even mention to my mom that I was with Hayley. I guess even she knew about my feelings for her.

"Yeah, the two of us kind of have a difference in opinion about my relationship with her."

"Oh Morgan, I'm sorry. Even I knew you were in love with his sister; that's why you never cared about being with anyone before. Well, I'm happy that you two are together, I just wished it was under better circumstances."

"Me too."

"Well, I won't keep you, since I know you shouldn't be on the phone too long."

I nodded. "You're right. This might be the last time we'll talk until I can figure out another way to reach out to you. But in the meantime, Aunt Doris will be coming by the house to check up on you."

"That's not necessary."

"Yes, it is. The two of you haven't seen in each other in years, so I'm sure she'll be happy to see you."

I could tell my mom was smiling through the phone as I had to smile myself. This was the first normal conversation we had in a long time, which felt pretty good.

"Can you at least tell me where you're going?"

I wanted to, but I didn't think it was wise.

"I can't, Mom, but trust me, I'll be in contact soon."

"Morgan, be careful. I love you."

"I love you too, Mom. I'll be in touch."

I didn't want to hang up, but we were on the phone for way too long. I disconnected, slowly putting it down and sighed.

"You okay?"

I looked over and saw Hayley wide awake.

I nodded as she sat up. "Yeah. It was kind of hard saying good-bye to my mom."

She looked sad as she put her arms around me. "I know it was difficult, especially since you're not sure when you'll speak with her again."

"Yeah, it was. I told her Doris would be looking after her. I texted her earlier to see if she could. It would be good for them to see each other and catch up."

"I agree. Your mom needs to be around family. Just like you need to."

I smiled. "Well, I am with you."

She smiled as I held her. "I still feel bad for putting you in this."

Hayley gave a small sigh while caressing my face. "You didn't force me to come. In fact, I was sort of begging."

"Yeah, you were definitely doing that, which was kind of sexy."

"Really, Morgan. I'm trying to be serious right now."

"I am too; but everything about you is sexy. You could be reciting the damn phone book and I'll be horny for you."

She shook her head. "I bet."

I lay down and gently pulled her to me. She lay down beside me while I stared at her.

"I really hope this is over soon."

"What if it's not?"

I shrugged. "Well, I guess the good thing is we'll be together."

She leaned over and kissed me.

I really did hope this would be over so I could go back to my normal routine. That, and I could rebuild the relationship I had with my mom. Just that conversation alone showed that it could be fixed, but I need to be there to do it. Once I was able to, that would be the first thing I would do.

27. Hayley

After getting some more needed rest, we were back on the road the next morning. Morgan wanted to drive straight through to Dallas so we could get there at a reasonable time. His uncle knew we were coming, so everything was set-up for us once we arrived.

Within three hours, we were pulling up into his driveway. I glanced at Morgan who took my hand.

"Are you going to keep the car now?"

"Maybe so; probably will get it painted and possibly see if it could be re-registered with a new license plate. How are you feeling?"

I smiled. "I'm okay. It's a new day, so everything is fine."

Morgan reached over and kissed me before we got out of the car. His uncle Rick and his wife Caroline came out of the house and greeted us both. As soon as we were about to enter the house, someone came into the driveway with his arms outstretched. I glanced at Morgan who had a huge grin.

"How are you?" The guy asked as he hugged Morgan.

"I'm great. Damn, I haven't seen you in years."

"I know. What brings you by?"

"Just visiting, since its Thanksgiving and all. Will, this is my girlfriend, Hayley. Hayley, my cousin, Will."

I smiled as I extended my hand out to Will, but instead, he put me in his arms to hug me. I felt a little awkward, but I guess he was friendly with everyone.

"Nice to meet you, Hayley. Anyone that Morgan knows is automatically good people."

"Thanks, Will."

He gave me a smile that made me a little uncomfortable. Actually, his entire demeanor was a little weird. Maybe I'm being paranoid, but I automatically didn't like him.

"Well, why don't you two get situated while we get ready for Thanksgiving dinner?" Caroline said as she gave me a pat on the back.

I nodded as Morgan took my hand. I glanced over and saw Will staring at me. I gave a light shiver as I followed Morgan into the house. Hopefully this visit would be a short one and everything could be resolved quickly, because for some reason, I didn't trust his cousin.

Not one bit...

28. Will

After everyone went inside, I quickly got my phone and hit talk. I needed to provide an update to what was happening.

When Morgan called my dad to let him know he was coming, I couldn't help but be a little excited, since that meant he would be close, and the plan could go on.

The other line picked up and the person started talking.

"Did you meet her?"

"Yeah. I didn't think she was going to arrive with Morgan, but she actually did."

"It's a good thing she did. Now, everything will go easier than we planned."

"Definitely. And Morgan won't know the wiser."

"No, he won't. Now, he'll know how it feels to lose someone that's special to him."

"Don't you think we should try and go after his mom?"

"No; too easy. Besides, Hayley is Lamar's sister, so it's like killing two birds with one stone."

I glanced over my shoulder to see if I was still alone. Sure enough, I was.

"Just don't screw this plan up. Even though he's your cousin, there's still a lot at stake. So, are you still with me on this?"

I sighed and ran a hand through my hair.

"Answer me, Will."

"Yes, I'm with you. In a few weeks, the plan will go into effect."

"Good. And I want updates. Even though we know enough about her, I need more information on Hayley Stevens."

"I know. I'll keep you posted."

"Good. Talk to you soon."

"Okay, Dad."

I hung up the phone and signed. Honestly, I didn't want to go through with this plan, but my dad was right; I needed to do this for my real father and for Uncle Craig.

I needed to put the person who killed him away for good.

And she didn't know it, but his little girlfriend was going to help me do it.

Music Playlist

The music playlist for *Something Just Ain't Right* is a great mix of songs that I believe describes the story between Haley and Morgan.

Shakira (Ft. Rhianna)- Can't Remember to Forget You

Kelly Rowland (Ft. Solange)- Simply Deep

Bruno Mars- Show Me

Beyonce- Blow

Maroon 5- It Was Always You

Maroon 5- Kiss Me

Nick Jonas- Jealous

Jessie J- Burning Up

Jennifer Hudson- Dangerous

David Guetta (Ft. Sam Martin)- Dangerous

K. Michelle- Going Under

Maroon 5 (Ft. Gwen Stefani) -My Heart Is Open

Kem.- Nobody

Keyshia Cole- I Remember (Part 2)

Arianna Grande (Ft. The Weeknd)- Love Me Harder

If you are a Spotify subscriber, check out the Something Just Ain't Right playlist, available now.

Other Books by Sheena Binkley

Available Now:

<u>In Love With My Best Friend series</u>
In Love With My Best Friend (Camille & Trevor)
A Chance at Love (Tia & Charles)
The Wedding Part I (Camille & Trevor)
The Wedding Part II (Tia & Charles)
<u>Love , Life, & Happiness series</u>
Love Unbroken (Riana & Shawn)
Trust Me (Cheryl & Marcus)
Unconditional Love (Britney & Jayden)
The Way We Were (Monica & Donnell)
Love Always (Riana & Shawn)
Redemption (Nathan)
Love, Life, & Happiness Christmas
<u>Something Just Ain't Right series (Hayley & Morgan)</u>
Something Just Ain't Right
Something Just Ain't Right 2
Something Just Ain't Right 3
Just Right (SJAR Novella)
<u>No Other Love series (Kevin, Carla, & Jennifer)</u>
No Other Love
No Other Love 2
No Other Love 3
<u>One Shot With A Baller series (Jayden & Zack)</u>
One Shot With A Baller- The Complete Series
<u>The Love Chronicles series (Andre & Dexter)</u>
The Love Chronicles
Say That You Love Me
How Deep Is Your Love
Love You For Life (Coming Soon)
<u>Into You series</u>
Into You (Vanessa & Mark)

Resisting Temptation (Reece & Troy)
<u>Love, Life, & Happiness: The Lost Story</u>
The Lost Story- Parts 1-4
<u>Reclaiming What Is Mine series (Asia & Bryon)</u>
Reclaiming What Is Mine
Reclaiming What Is Ours
<u>Lessons In Love series</u>
Lessons In Love (Trina)
<u>Standalone Books</u>
Our Love (Charlie & Michael)
The Evolution Of Love (Elise, Jared, & Dante)
Love & Drama: The Root Of All Evil (Zuri & Damon)
I'm The Only One You Need (Mika, Devin, & Anthony)
Real Love (Riana & Shawn)
Believe In Love (Cheryl & Marcus)
Lady Guardians: The Ultimate Risk (Raven & Ryan)

About the Author

Sheena Binkley first discovered her love for storytelling when writing her first story for a class project at the tender age of nine. Since then, she has composed several short stories and numerous tales that are not only engaging, but simply entertaining. She is also a freelance writer, penning articles on various topics including education and entertainment.

To date, her best-selling novels include In Love With My Best Friend, Love Unbroken, Something Just Ain't Right, and The Love Chronicles.

In April of 2016, Sheena launched her own publishing company which focus strictly on romance books. Besides writing, she loves reading, shopping, and spending time with family and friends. She lives in Houston (where the weather is always unpredictable) with her husband and son.

Email: sheenabinkley@live.com

Goodreads: www.goodreads.com/authorSheenaBinkley

Blog: http://sheenabinkley.com/

Facebook: www.facebook.com/sheenabinkleyauthor (Like Page)

Twitter: @ChevonBink

Google +: https://plus.google.com/+sheenabinkley

Pinterest: Sheena Binkley

Facebook Group: https://www.facebook.com/groups/ 577100099053119/?fref=ts

Mailing List: http://eepurl.com/bY22E9

Don't miss out!

Visit the website below and you can sign up to receive emails whenever Sheena Binkley publishes a new book. There's no charge and no obligation.

https://books2read.com/r/B-A-XOUF-RRAMB

BOOKS 2 READ

Connecting independent readers to independent writers.